# Victoria's Run

## A Novel

## CHERYL HOLDEFER

Printed in the United States of America

*Victoria's Run*

Copyright © 2013 by Cheryl Holdefer
Cover Design by Sarah Hansen
Okaycreations.net
Formatting: JT Formatting
www.facebook.com/JTFormatting

ISBN-13: 978-0615774886
ISBN-10: 0615774881

*To Lauren and Ricky, my children:*
*I am so proud of whom you have become!*
*I love you with all my heart.*

# CHAPTER ONE

"Chris, come here!" she exclaimed to her older brother.

"What is it, Jen?" he answered impatiently.

"I need you to look at something. Just for one second!"

"I'm busy writing this term paper for college."

"Please, Chris? I think you'll find it interesting," she pleaded.

Her brother walked into the laundry room where she was sitting on the floor surrounded by boxes of papers and old yearbooks. He was annoyed because he wanted to finish writing his term paper. This was his last semester of college and he just wanted it to be over. No more books, no more tests, no more term papers. Jennifer was in her last year of high school, so she couldn't possibly understand his frustration with college professors who believed that only *their* class mattered. But he adored his little sister and would do anything for her.

"What?" he asked, sighing heavily.

"This is something I found, and I think you should read it. I'll tell you why after you read it. It's a story."

"I can see that."

"Just read it, please?"

### The Jacket

*It had been a rough year of agonizing soul-searching that ended with a decision that should have been made a long time ago. She had certainly made some poor choices in love earlier in her life, but now she wondered at the age of forty-three how she had once again been in a relationship that had ended after spending four years of her life trying to make it work. She had debated all year whether or not to continue down the road that neither one of them had secretly believed would lead to a future life together. And yet, they had stayed together. It had been comfortable. Convenient.*

*She wondered how many other women stayed in dead-end relationships for the same reasons. And men, for that matter. It was certainly complicated. How do you leave someone you really enjoy being with, but you know it isn't the kind of glue, of love and commitment, that keeps you connected for the long term?*

*She was now at a point in her life when she was able to reflect on her mistakes and choices and face the challenges of her future. Perhaps it would be a future in which she would have to be alone, but she would create a fulfilling happy one. She had always been a positive person in the past, and she could be that dormant person again. She couldn't turn back the clock and regain lost time or correct her mistakes, but she could make sure she would not make them again.*

*On this particular afternoon, she had wanted to be alone for a while to think about her next steps. Perhaps a career change. Perhaps she would look into buying a new car. Maybe she would just adopt a dog. She wandered aimlessly into a restaurant not too far from her home. She had heard that if you wanted to be alone, your best bet would be to hide yourself in a crowd. She walked through the door of the restaurant and suddenly felt quite vulnerable. She quickly decided not to approach the bar. Bars were for people who were searching for other people; for people who were waiting despairingly for some stranger to walk up and change their lives. Not her. No, a small table by the window would be just fine, she decided. She ordered a dry white wine at room temperature. She didn't like confusing the buttery oak taste of a wine by the cold temperature of refrigeration.*

*She stared out of the window beside her table, thinking about nothing in particular; simply watching others as the details of her own life passed by unobtrusively. She pressed her face closer to the window pane and strained to see the children outside by the pond in front of the restaurant. Some were feeding the geese and some were just running back and forth flapping their wings and laughing. A smile crossed her face. It felt good to be alive.*

*Suddenly a reflection of someone behind her appeared in the glass, disrupting her thoughts and arousing her curiosity. She turned and looked at the tall man's back as he passed by her and walked towards the bar.*

*The man hesitated for a moment, wondering whether he should approach the group of people chatting mindlessly at the end of the bar, or if he should take a table of his own. No table, he decided. A table for one gave the impression of loneliness, of desperation, as if you were waiting for someone who would never appear. He sat on a stool towards the middle of the counter and ordered a beer.*

*She stared at the back of his head covered with soft brown hair. He turned slowly and stood up to take off his jacket. She noticed his lean body as he stood, but was struck by his face. He had sharp blue eyes that infused into the depths of her soul and pervaded her with such intensity that it caused her to gasp and quickly look away. She was sure that he could conjure anger, fear, or the most uncontrollable desire with those impenetrable blue eyes! His upper lip curved with unintended lust when he broke into a smile as he ordered his beer.*

*Who was he? Who was this man that walked into this non-descript place with such an unassuming step and unabashed confidence? What sort of man wore a brown leather jacket with such indifference? A professor? A runner? A racecar driver? He slowly placed the jacket on the back of his seat. She then noticed the flight wings on the left shoulder of the jacket. Underneath he was wearing a soft white wool sweater.*

*She watched as he eventually finished the onion soup he had ordered, and she her ham on rye. Then he maneuvered off the barstool, left some money on the counter, and turned to leave.*

*"Don't forget your jacket," she heard herself say.*

*Their eyes locked for a moment. She didn't know whether she*

3

*had actually said 'Don't forget your jacket,' or 'don't forget me.' But it had only been the jacket, she concluded, as he lifted it off the stool and turned towards the door. Their eyes met once more as he passed by her table. Her breathing suspended and the silence resounded loudly in her ears. The moments he stood there felt like forever. She had so many questions for him; so many thoughts to share. But she had said nothing, and he turned, and walked out the door.*

*'Would you like to join me for a glass of wine?' she could have asked. But she hadn't. He was gone.*

*"I could have loved you," she whispered softly, and stared out the window at the children and geese beyond.*

"So what do you make of it, Chris?" asked Jennifer.

"It's good," he responded. "Nice short story." He handed her the papers as he stood and walked away.

"Chris," she said trailing behind him. "I didn't write it. I think Mom did, and I think these men could have existed in her life. I mean, why else would she write it? Did mom have a boyfriend after she and dad split up?"

"How would I know?" Chris was already headed back to the den.

"No, really! Look at the date. There's a date at the bottom of the last page. It says that it was written two years ago. It doesn't make sense, though, because I found it in that box with all her old papers and yearbooks from college. But it might be about someone she dated after dad. Or maybe she's dating him now, and we don't even know about it!"

"Your imagination is getting the best of you, Jen."

Chris didn't really need to know where his sister had found the story, or what the date had been, because he already knew as soon as he had started reading the story that it could have only been written by their mother about someone she had in fact known not too long ago. It all made sense now. It wasn't about the man that had confused her with his lack of commitment. He didn't exist. It was about the man in the bar. Chris remembered the leather brown jacket with the pilot's wings on the left shoulder. He had seen it on someone years ago, and now it all started to...

"I found it in her college yearbook, by the way," his sister said, coming back into the den and leaning over her brother's shoulder as he typed at his computer.

"What? Oh. Well, I'm sure mom wrote it during her college days for some English class or something and then tucked it away in the yearbook and forgot about it."

Temporarily satisfied with his answer, Jennifer retreated back into the laundry room to continue rummaging through the box of yearbooks and pictures she had found earlier.

Chris sat at his computer, but his thoughts were not on his work. A few minutes later, Jennifer emerged from the laundry room once again.

"The date, Chris. What about the date?"

"Jen, you are relentless! Don't you have any place to go? Any little friends to play with outside?" He gently pushed her aside and tried to concentrate on his typing.

"Christopher Taylor! Don't you treat me like some little kid! I am eighteen years old and I can beat you at any sport you name, by the way!"

"Jennifer! We're *late!*" her mother's voice came trailing down the stairs.

"Coming, mom!" she yelled back. "Shit, Chris, why didn't you tell me what time it was?! I'm late for softball! Oh well, they'll just have to wait for me!"

Jennifer quickly kissed her brother on the head, turned, and bound up the stairway leaving her long blonde hair to trail behind. She grabbed her gym bag by the front door and ran out to the waiting car.

"Okay, mom, GO!"

"Aren't you forgetting something?"

"No," she said with commitment. Then after a moment, "Okay, what am I forgetting?"

Victoria pointed to her daughter's hand.

"My glove! Crap! Wait for me, mom!"

*No*, Victoria thought with a smile on her face as she shook her head from side to side. No, she would not wait for her impetuous daughter. She would go to the softball game without her absent-minded, yet bright, witty, and very popular daughter. *Too* popular, she thought. Jennifer was way too busy for a girl her age. For years her daughter had been involved in myriad activities including the softball team, the equestrian team, the cross country team, co-ed volleyball, and tennis. She had tried it all. She skied in the winter and swam in the summer. She had a creative edge as well, and her most recent drawings of penguins had been displayed at the local community center. Her music teacher extolled her talent at the piano and urged her to abandon the frivolous idea of playing sports. As if that were not enough, her English teacher had asked her to try out for the spring play. But Victoria had drawn the line at that point, and convinced her daughter that rehearsals would have consumed the very limited time she had had remaining. After all, where would friends and shopping and dating fit in?

Jennifer seemed to be able to handle all of her activities, though, and still maintain grades that kept her on the honor roll. No one in the family had ever pressured her to excel and perform as she did. She was just driven, and she was a natural. Victoria wasn't quite sure where her daughter's talent had come from, even though she herself had attempted to play the piano and study art when she was young. But her own talent had never been explored nor developed past the ninth grade. Victoria's parents had divorced when she was very young, and neither parent had been able to afford lessons of any kind. Instead, Victoria had concentrated on sports. Well, on one sport: running. Running hadn't cost any money.

Victoria thought back to those days when she had been as eager as her daughter is now. She had loved running! By the time she had returned from living with her father in Denmark for two years to live with her mother in Puerto Rico at the age of 14, Victoria had already been running distances for one year. Soon after she had returned to the island, she had vowed to run its entire length, from one side of the island to the other. Why not? After all, Puerto Rico measured only one hundred miles by thirty five miles! She had believed she was invincible, much like Jennifer believes now.

Victoria remembered how she used to be called '*la rubia*' on the island, in spite of the fact that she had never been a blonde at all like Jennifer; she had light brown hair. Oh well. It hadn't been her hair that made the people on the island take notice, it had been her raw determination to run faster and further each day as she ventured out into the streets. The locals had been observing this determined spirit as she ran the same routes each morning. She had run barefoot much of the time. In those early days of running, Victoria hadn't owned a pair of real running shoes. The companies weren't making them for women, and the men's shoes were so big and heavy! Eventually she did get a pair of shoes, but they were so heavy that she had ended up taking them off mid-way through her run. She had been teased about running with those shoes on her hands instead of on her feet, but it was those shoes that got her into college and...

"Found it!" exclaimed Jennifer as she jumped into the car and slammed the door. "Okay, GO!"

*Yes*, thought Victoria, her daughter was definitely more impetuous than she had ever been as a youngster. Victoria had only wanted to run the length of an island, but Jennifer would probably run half-way around the world if her mother would let her!

"Mom?"

7

"Yes dear?"

"I've been curious about your track record when you were in college. You know, to see how we two compare? So I dug out your old yearbooks and running logs that you keep in that box of college stuff in the laundry room."

"Cool!" Victoria responded. "We'll have to look at those old charts after dinner tonight, you think?"

There was no mention of the story. Maybe she had forgotten it was in one of the boxes, Jennifer thought.

"So why all the sudden inquisitiveness about my track record?" Victoria mused as she rushed through a yellow traffic light anxiously trying to get her daughter to the game on time. The softball coach had a way of admonishing the girls with his silent treatment, and they always feared being benched for the game if they crossed him too much. They knew that tardiness was an infraction the whole team would have to pay for after the game by running continuous laps around the field. Victoria would like to see that coach carry his big gut around that diamond just once after the game.

"To compare," Jennifer said.

"To compare what, sweetie?"

"I wanted to see your records so that I could compare them to mine. You know, to see if people in the olden days could run as fast as we can today."

"*Olden days?!*" Victoria laughed out loud. "So what did you discover about us old dried up athletes? How do we compare to you young ones in the twenty first century?"

"Well, I never got around to looking at your records. But I did discover something," replied Jennifer.

"And what would that be?"

"I found a story." She waited. No reaction. Okay, no turning back now, thought Jennifer. "Who wrote *The Jacket*, mom? Was it you?" Jennifer glanced at her mom carefully, not knowing what to expect.

*"The Jacket,"* Victoria repeated, and retreated into silence.

Perhaps this hadn't been such a good time to ask her mom, thought Jennifer. Timing is everything, and timing things correctly was certainly not her forte.

Judiciously she ventured on. "Yeah, the story about two people passing each other in a bar. Was it a true story?"

"I wrote it a long time ago," mumbled Victoria. Jennifer thought about the date recorded below the story, but she decided against mentioning it for the moment.

"Was it true?" she pushed.

"Your grandfather once told me that one should write as if writing the pages of a diary. Emulate reality and throw in a twist of the surreal. Mirror people you know, he said, and write the pages of your life, your dreams, and your misfortunes."

The car screeched to a halt at the softball field forcing Jennifer to end the conversation.

"Aha!" exclaimed Victoria, "We have landed! Now, get out there fast and hope that Coach hasn't noticed your absence!"

"Mom, I'm the pitcher," she sighed and rolled her eyes in amusement, "so I don't think I can just slither into the dugout!"

Victoria walked towards the stands away from the girls who were now moaning as they suffered through another of the coach's interminable speeches about laziness, lack of appreciation for softball, and whatever else the coach felt obligated to unload on his rookies as he instilled discipline disguised as team spirit. The coach would later credit a win to his inspiring speech, or he'd blame a loss on the lack of team effort or not attending to his signals out on the field. The fact was that the girls could barely understand his signals, because half the time he just made them up.

Today Victoria didn't stop at the stands where the other parents ceremoniously gathered for idle yet pleasant dribble. Instead she veered off towards a clump of trees with a pad of paper and pen in hand and she sat where she could see the game yet avoid having to talk to anyone else.

*"The Jacket,"* she silently repeated to herself. Two years had seemed so long ago. How had it all started? She began to recall a series of events that had made a lasting impact on her life, from her days growing up in Puerto Rico and Denmark where she fell in love with running, to her Olympic marathon training days, and to the day she met her coach, Dan Cole, the man in the brown leather jacket.

# CHAPTER TWO

Victoria Richards thought back to the days of her childhood when she had been an introverted yet happy child growing up. Her father and mother had married young without really knowing each other very well. Her father, Jack, had proposed to Rebecca through a missive while serving his term in the Navy on a destroyer in the South Pacific during World War II. It had been the thing to do in those days, marry one's sweetheart during war time. Many of those marriages worked out. Some of them did not.

Rebecca had married Jack at the age of 21, had a miscarriage the following year, and two years later they were headed for a divorce. When she discovered she was pregnant with Victoria right before the divorce, Rebecca put in a concerted effort to save the marriage. By the time Victoria was six months old, however, the marriage had crumbled beyond repair. Jack was devastated, but he eventually recuperated, remarried, and moved to Europe as a struggling journalist with a new wife and a baby on the way. Rebecca met and later married another serviceman, Antonio Velasco, who had been stationed at the Air Force base in Tucson, Arizona, where she lived. They soon moved to Puerto Rico where he had been born and raised, and they had two more daughters.

Victoria was seven-years-old when she landed in Puerto Rico with her mom and step-dad, and even at that young age she had been struck by the island's natural beauty. There were sights and adventures to capture the heart of any child. The streets were narrow and clean and they wound in and out of small neighborhoods with beautiful white houses surrounded by bright bold flowers. There were banana, avocado, and mango trees every-where. *Bouganvilia* and brilliant *amapolas* the size of her fists adorned windowsills throughout the neighborhoods and spilled off the balconies onto the cobble streets below. There were metal slats for the windows, *porcianas,* which would be cranked open to let in the air on the oppressively humid days of the summer. The temperature generally hovered around 98 degrees in the summer, and it was mostly in the 70's during the winter. Some people had screens on their windows, but Victoria's family had not been able afford them. They had used mosquito nets to cover their beds at night, and they would fold them up and tuck them under their pillows during the day. Since the windows were always open, though, the lizards would wander in at leisure and explore the walls, the showers, and the insides of shoes.

The floors of Victoria's small home had been the coolest place to sit, she remembered, because the tiles did not absorb the heat. The furniture in the living room was made of bamboo with plastic cushions, because wood and fabric never fared too well with the *salitre* in the air, the salt from the Caribbean Sea. As a matter of fact, cars never lasted very long either because the hoods would start rusting within a year of their purchase. There were so many old abandoned cars on the island that they had to be buried underground.

The sewage system at Victoria's little home on the island had never quite worked as it should have, she recalled, and the stench of human waste that sometimes seeped out into their front yard when the pipes got backed up underground had been almost unbearable. Sometimes after a storm, the water from the spigots had looked more like mud than water, but people just ignored it and boiled whatever they needed for drinking. They would shower in that water twice each day, only because it was so unpleasantly humid outside.

Victoria smiled as she thought to herself that you were *no one*, really, if you didn't own a cow or a pig or at least some chickens in your back yard. Chickens had roamed freely in Victoria's neighborhood, and they had truly lived a life of leisure. Chickens were allowed in the houses. They could even ride from town to town on the *guagua*, or bus. Victoria had owned a chicken when she was young too: Paquito. It would lazily meander throughout the neighborhood and around the house during the daytime, but at night it had insisted on sleeping in a tree. So before bedtime each evening, Victoria would have to put Paquito in a tree. God forbid it should fall out in the middle of the night! Then Paquito disappeared one night. Victoria recalled sending all her little friends out into the neighborhood to see if anyone was eating chicken soup the next day.

Victoria had always felt that the *puertoriqueños* were a loving, protective, and respectful people. They had cared for her mom and her siblings without hesitation, even though Rebecca had never quite learned to speak their language very well. Victoria would never forget the day when her mother's small black Renault exploded into flames from overheating, and a man jumped out of his own car, took off his *guayavera,* and put out the flames with his shirt. He had no money to help them get on a bus, but he walked out into the middle of the road and hailed a cab driver, exchanged words briefly in Spanish, and the driver took them to where they needed to go without charging them a penny. They had been headed to Boquerón.

Victoria pondered that those first few years on the island had been difficult years of adjustment for her parents. She recalled the arguments that took place around corners in hushed voices, mostly about money. On top of it all, Rebecca didn't speak Spanish, so it had been difficult to assimilate and to find a job. Antonio, Victoria's stepfather, had spent years in the army and had not been prepared for the world of work. But he was an industrious and conscientious person, so he eventually found a way to raise the children and support the family. Through the recommendation of a cousin of a friend of his own cousin, he began working for a reputable insurance company. He was a good agent. He learned quickly. He was also extremely honest, a quality his clients appreciated, even though it kept him from getting those larger commissions that could have helped his family so desperately.

In the meantime, Puerto Rico had appeared to be prospering right around the time they had moved there. Mr. Truman's *Operation Bootstrap* in 1952 began the industrialization of this predominantly agricultural island that had been captured by US forces in the Spanish-American War. Beautiful new hotels were built to accommodate the increasing amount of tourists each year and to house the corporate teams that benefited from *Section 936 of the US Internal Revenue Code*, legislation that gave large tax credits on profits earned by American manufacturers and their subsidiaries functioning on the island. Initially the controversial tax incentive had given Puerto Rico one of the highest standards of living in Latin America. Two thousand factories had eventually migrated to the island and employed over 100,000 citizens. But the island never could have predicted the darkened days when decades later an American president would eliminate their corporate welfare as an anti-poverty measure under the guise of making them self-sufficient again. There would be no federal incentives for the new investments, and the factories would shut down.

Earlier on, however, the American factories had lured the farmers and their children away from working the crops, and there was money to make working in those factories. The younger generation began to quickly depend on the Industrialists with a renewed hope and vision for their future. The uneducated farmer became an unskilled worker in a factory without a union and without a set wage. But there was food on the table every night, and the children had shoes. An island that had been predominantly agricultural and self-sufficient became an industrialized and largely dependent country.

Victoria's stepfather had benefited from the impassioned conversion as well. As the top executives moved to the island to oversee their subsidiaries, the insurance demands grew. The *jíbaros* from the mountains and the unskilled laborers could not afford to buy insurance. The money simply was not there. But the mainlanders believed in buying insurance, especially when cautioned about the hurricane season and its ravenous appetite for expensive beach houses owned by foreigners. Fear grasped them all when the hurricanes threatened to rip the heart out of the island. Windows were boarded, furniture was tied down, pools were emptied, and cars were chained to the ground. All the containers in the houses were filled with water in case a *sequía* or water shortage followed the storm. Telephone communication was halted by the government. Stores were sold out of flashlights, batteries, and canned goods. Cat and dog food disappeared from the shelves as well, even though domestic pets were a rarity in most homes. In the midst of all the confusion, the islanders were adept and knew exactly what to do and what to expect because hurricanes were such a common experience. The locals would help all the visitors on the island, because that was the type of people they were. Victoria especially appreciated the hurricane season because she knew that her stepfather would be very busy selling insurance and collecting commissions. That meant that there would be meat to go with the spaghetti, and her mother would bake cookies and buy some big shiny bottles of *Royal Crown Cola*.

Eventually Antonio had managed to buy an old Renault from a brother-in-law of a cousin. Or maybe it wasn't a cousin. In any case, the car had enabled Rebecca to find a job with a small but promising newspaper, *The San Juan Star,* which was published daily in Spanish and in English for the growing number of northerners who continued to immigrate to the Caribbean. Rebecca worked as an administrative secretary. Her meager wages, along with Antonio's commissions, eventually made it possible for the family to buy their first little house instead of renting. It wasn't much, Victoria reflected, but it was theirs. Victoria had shared a room with her two sisters, Rina and little Esperanza. These had been happy times.

Esperanza, whose name translated to *Hope,* had been an ebullient little child full of energy. She made everyone laugh and kept everyone in good physical shape as they vigorously chased after her up and down the streets of the neighborhood. Rina had been the quieter sibling, until you got to know her. Rina was talented in every sense of the word. She was a natural athlete, extremely artistic, and had a melodious voice that mesmerized everyone who heard her sing. Victoria was the oldest child, so naturally it was she who had cared for her half-sisters while Rebecca and Antonio were at work.

During the school year, a neighbor would watch over little Esperanza until the two older siblings came home. Victoria was five years older than Rina and six years older than Esperanza. On those afternoons after school, Victoria reminisced, she would help Rina with her homework, wash her sisters' uniforms for the next day, and start dinner. She would also bail Esperanza out if she was up to her mischievous little pranks when Antonio called on the phone from work to check in on them. Rebecca would come home from work in the evenings at different times, depending on Antonio's schedule, since he drove the only car that they owned. If Antonio had been with a client, they both knew that the prospect of a commission was important, so Rebecca would have to wait for him to pick her up when he had finished with the meeting. Rebecca would read borrowed books from her colleagues at work as she'd sit outside on the curb in front of the building waiting for her husband. She had always worried about the children on those late afternoons. She had relied so much on Victoria to keep things together.

Victoria thought about the time that her mom had especially become worried about little Esperanza. Esperanza had been complaining intermittingly about stomach pains over a period of several months. Victoria tried to remember exactly when this was, but things were so fuzzy now. She recalled that one day her mom had been so worried that she had carried Esperanza for three miles to the free clinic in their small town while Antonio was at work, and that the doctor had told her mom that Esperanza's stomach pains were probably from indigestion, maybe an allergy, or maybe even growing pains. You couldn't tell with Esperanza, because she was always so happy.

But then Rebecca had found out just how sick Esperanza really was. While she had waited to be picked up after work by Antonio one evening, one of her co-workers had run hastily down the steps and out to the parking lot to tell Rebecca that Esperanza had taken a fall and was being driven to the hospital near their home by a neighbor. She had injured her chin and would probably need some stitches. Not too serious, the colleague had reported; just the stitches. Rebecca had tried unsuccessfully to reach Antonio by phone inside the building for about an hour. Victoria wished now that cell phones had been invented back in those days. There had been no answer at her father's office, so her mom had assumed he was out on the road with a client. Resigned, Rebecca had asked if a co-worker could take her to the hospital in Bayamón. Victoria had already enlisted the help of a neighbor, Don Julio, to take her and her two little sisters to the hospital so a doctor could look at Esperanza's chin while her mom continued trying to get a ride.

Rebecca had arrived at the hospital at around 6 pm, nearly two hours after the accident, to find little Esperanza cradled in Victoria's arms in a chair in the waiting room. A bloodied towel was under her chin. Rina was huddled next to the neighbor Don Julio. He explained to Rebecca that Esperanza's case had been considered to be less serious by the nurses than some of the others, so they were still waiting for assistance. The teary-eyed Esperanza held out her little arms for her mother as they were finally summoned into the doctor's office.

"*Tengo sueñito*" she had said to her mother. "I'm sleepy." Those words still echoed in Victoria's mind after all these years.

"I know, sweetie" Rebecca had said. "You can sleep soon when *papito* comes to take us home. First we must see the doctor."

Antonio had gone to pick up his wife at six o'clock at the *Star* and had been informed that he had just missed her. When Antonio arrived at the hospital forty-five minutes later, he found Rebecca listening intently to Dr. Ramirez as they stood outside of the door to the treatment room. The doctor explained that he had sewn five little stitches into Esperanza's chin, which had been a simple process in itself, but that he was more worried about her unusually high temperature than the cut on her chin. After numerous questions about her recent complaints of stomach pains, the doctor had decided to keep Esperanza at the hospital overnight for observation.

Esperanza never came home from the hospital. She was buried on a rainy Tuesday one month later.

"The sky is crying," Rebecca had told her two daughters as she had held them close at the funeral protecting them from the gentle rain…

Victoria believed to this day that she had been to blame for her little sister's death. She knew in her logical mind that there was nothing she could have done to prevent her sister's illness. Yet she couldn't help thinking that she should have watched over her more carefully. She should have known something was wrong. Esperanza had always been so energetic and playful. Victoria remembered clearly the image of one day when she had chased after her little sister to give her a bath, and Esperanza had climbed up the concrete blocks on the side of the carport and onto the roof of the house in order to get away from her! She recalled how on another day she had found her little sister hiding under her bed with her mother's red lipstick all over her clothes and face. Those were precious memories. But Victoria chided herself for not realizing then that something had been wrong when little Esperanza had become so languid those last few months of her life.

Victoria thought about how Esperanza had died right before her fifth birthday. Victoria, Rina, and her mom had been planning a little party for her. Victoria remembered how she had been so excited because she had made a bright yellow and orange kite for her sister. She thought about how she later had sat there and cried for hours holding onto that kite after her sister's death. Rina was only a year older than Esperanza at the time, but she had shared in the despair of her eleven-year-old sister as they grieved and watched their parents slowly fall apart in the ensuing months after Esperanza's death.

Antonio had been devastated. Victoria learned later that her step-father had felt terrible guilt, just as she had. He had been angry that he was so busy selling his damned insurance policies that he had not even listened to Esperanza's complaints about her stomach pains. He hadn't noticed the changes in his little girl's weight. He had thought that she had the flu. He felt that he could have saved her life. She could have had her birthday party. Esperanza could have grown up to be a lawyer or a dentist. She would have fallen in love someday, and he would have walked her down the aisle at her wedding. But instead of giving her away at the altar, he had given her away to God. On that one night in the hospital, he had allowed her to slip away into a permanent repose while he had been holding her weak little body tenderly in his arms. She had said she was going to sleep. Those were the words. He had held her well into the morning stroking her hair and whispering prayers to her as if breath still lingered in that small lifeless body in his arms.

Rebecca had awoken in her chair next to Esperanza's bed where Antonio had been holding her, and she had gone into shock. She was sedated for several days after the death of her child, but then she regained the control she had needed when everyone around her had seemingly lost direction. Rebecca was the mother, and she had known that she had to take care of the family. There were two little girls who still needed their mother, and it was up to her to reassure them that Esperanza was in heaven with lots of little angels and that someday they would see her again when the time was right.

"*Mamá, hay caramelitos en el cielo?*" Rina had asked.

"Yes, there is plenty of candy in Heaven."

Rina had seemed placated with this answer, fully believing that Esperanza was getting a pretty good deal.

Antonio, however, could not be conciliated. He had agreed to meet with the priest at Rebecca's urging, but just as he would not speak to anyone in the family, he would speak to the priest least of all. He fell deeper and deeper into depression and he began to drink and stay out late at night at the local *tabernas*. Rebecca had continually answered phone calls from the bartenders in the middle of the night asking her to come and pick up her husband. Sometimes he would be quietly delivered home by a sympathetic *compadre*.

"*Señora?*" came the masculine voice over the phone one night.

"Yes?" Rebecca had replied, annoyed that once again she had had to wake up, dress, and drive out to some bar to pick up her inebriated husband.

"It is Antonio, *Señora*."

"Yes, I know, Don Rafael. Where do I pick him up this time?" She had recognized the bartender's voice.

"He has been in a car accident, *Señora*. Antonio is dead."

# CHAPTER THREE

It had been Victoria's twelfth birthday when her father Jack had called her on the phone all the way from Denmark to wish her well. It had been almost a year since her sister and step-father's deaths. Jack had been working in Europe for *Fairchild Publications* as a Bureau Chief when his daughter had been in Puerto Rico with her mom quietly suffering through her losses. As Jack spoke to Victoria and listened to all her stories from the previous year, he had gotten caught up in the moment and had asked her to come and live with him and his family in Denmark for a year. His son Steven was anxious to meet his half-sister. Jack had not seen Victoria since the day she had left with her mother for Puerto Rico and he had left with his new wife for Europe.

Rebecca had been furious that Jack had made the invitation without consulting her first. She had been caught off guard when Victoria had asked her if she could go and live with her father. Victoria was still fragile, and Rebecca did not want to let go of her. This also happened right around the time that Rebecca had been thinking about packing up and moving back to the States with her two daughters. After all, Antonio was gone, she could not speak Spanish, so it made sense to return to the States where she could find a better job, had a sister, and still had a few remaining friends in Arizona. She had wanted it to be a smooth transition for the girls. She certainly hadn't wanted to separate them, since Rina was Antonio's daughter and would not be going to live with Jack.

Rebecca had tried to explain to Jack that Antonio and Esperanza's deaths had profoundly affected Victoria, and that she felt her daughter needed to stay with her and Rina and maybe even try to get some professional help. There weren't too many therapists in Puerto Rico during those days, because it wasn't a concept that the culture embraced. It was perceived as a weakness to have to go to a therapist, and a frivolous expense at that. But perhaps if she moved back to the States, she could find help. Rebecca told Jack that Victoria had seemingly lost interest in her studies, her friends and her activities. She had become more introverted. She shared that she had entered her daughter's room one evening to find her sitting in a corner on the floor sobbing with her knees tucked tightly under her chin and Rina by her side saying "Don't worry, Vicky. We can see her in Heaven, and we'll share our toys with her." Rebecca had sat there quietly with her arms wrapped around both of her daughters and feeling helpless. Victoria had never been big on verbalizing her feelings, but she had always seemed like a happy child. Now a very different little girl seemed to be living behind the deep dark windows of Victoria's eyes. Victoria shouldn't have had to endure such tragedy in her short lifetime. Rebecca had wondered what *normal* would ever look like in her daughter's future. Hopefully Rina had been too young to understand fully what had happened.

But shortly after Jack had called and invited Victoria to visit, Rebecca had found one of her daughter's little poems lying on the floor underneath her bed when she went in to clean her room. Rebecca read it to herself and knew then that she must allow her daughter to go and see her father. And so she did.

*Echoes*
*Always hiding.*
*Always a storm.*
*I hear the waves rising,*
*I quietly close the door.*
*"Daddy!" I yell. "Daddy!"*
*My words become echoes*
*Far, far away.*
*I hide in the tempest*
*With nothing to say.*

# CHAPTER FOUR

Denmark had been exactly as Victoria's father had described it over the phone---COLD! It was as beautiful as she had pictured from the books by Hans Christian Andersen; books that she had checked out of the library before her trip. It was lush and green during the short months of the summer solstice and overwhelmingly cold during the long months of the winter. The cold weather in the winter had never seemed to particularly bother anyone who lived in Denmark. The people expected it, prepared for it, and dealt with it.

The Danes were precise, punctual people. They wore severe insolent faces as they rode their bikes or caught the train to work each morning. But their acrimonious countenance was simply a façade; they were actually quite friendly and informal. Their familiar tone even carried over to the educational system where students addressed their teachers by their first names. The Danes were intelligent and cognizant people who strived to be productive and to flourish in a wearisome and forgotten socialism. They were kind, composed, and possessed a cunning sense of humor and irony. There was much to learn from the Danish, Victoria had decided as a young girl, and so she ventured out of her depression from the previous year of her life in Puerto Rico to explore this self-confident society.

In Denmark Victoria had attended Rygaards Franske Skole, a private Christian and Catholic co-educational school that had two *Departments*, a Danish one and an International one. Victoria had attended the International Department and took her classes in French. It seemed to be the logical thing to do, since she had already been learning Spanish for five years and she thought the two languages might be similar. She loved the school. She would ride a bus from her father's apartment in Bagsværd to Lyngby Station every day, and then a train from Lyngby to Hellerup, an attractive suburb about fifteen minutes north of Copenhagen. She would walk to the eighteenth century schoolhouse from Hellerup station and would come through the back gates and enter the school through the gardens. She was one of about three hundred students from ages four to sixteen in the school. The International Department had generally catered to students who were in the country on a temporary basis. Since the curriculum was based on the British System with their standardized tests, Victoria had felt that she would have no problem returning to the school system in Puerto Rico the following year. That is, if her mother was still living on the island and hadn't returned to the States.

Victoria's school in Denmark was quite different than the one in Puerto Rico. On the island she remembered that *Colegio Espiritu Santo* didn't have a gymnasium for physical education, so the students would just do exercises in the courtyard. At the *Skole* they had two gymnasiums with clean polished wooden floors, ropes hanging from the ceiling, and ladders on the walls. There was some kind of contraption with two large rings hanging from the ceiling, and students would grab them and hang upside-down on them. Students would also run and jump over something called a *horse*. There was equipment Victoria had never seen before, and after the first day of gymnastics class, she had never wanted to see it again. The coach had a whistle, she recalled, and every time he blew that whistle, the students had to alternate between running, jumping jacks, and dropping to do push-ups. Then they would work on the equipment again. After a week of physical pain, Victoria had felt like the pain in her heart had met its match in her body. It felt good. She felt stronger. She was going to be in control again. She started running after school with two of her classmates, Hillary and Carole. She also learned to ice-skate, to work a tobog-gan, to ski, to race a bike, and of course to climb trees. She had decided that running was the most fun activity of all, and she had asked the teacher in gym if she could be placed in the boys' group for all the races. She had been determined to run as far and as fast as she could to gain control and to get ahead of her past. The hopelessness would disappear. And that would be that.

It was during this year in the seventh grade that Victoria met Gabrielle, and she became her dearest friend to the present day. Gabrielle was from France and had been living in Denmark where her father had been serving as an ambassador to the country. Gabrielle and Victoria had been assigned seats next to each other in their mathematics class, and that was how they had met. Gabrielle was an extrovert in every sense of the word, and Victoria was somewhat of an introvert keeping her most important thoughts private. At first, the two girls had had nothing in common except for their poor grades in math and their interest in art. Gabrielle was going to be a famous painter one day, and Victoria was going to be a famous athlete who appreciated good art. Victoria remembered how they would spend hours poring over books about artists, particularly Picasso. They had memorized every detail of every period in his life and they could name all of his mistresses. They had examined every angle of Françoise Gilot and Dora Maar in his paintings and had tried to figure out what pieces of them were missing in his cubistic renditions of their beauty and spirit. The girls had learned a lot about each other as they discussed and danced through his rose and blue periods. It was certainly unusual that girls their age had talked about art. But a bond was formed.

Victoria had tried every now and then to reveille in Gabrielle an interest in running with her and her two friends, but her attempts to convince her dearest friend to join them in the physical feat were politely refuted each time. Nonetheless, all four girls found a way to connect and spend time with each other. Sometimes Gabrielle would slowly peddle her bike around the castle at Bagsværd Lake while Victoria and her friends would run beside her. Or Gabrielle would set up her easel and paints to interpret the beauty of the old abandoned castle, while Victoria ran along the paths nearby. The girls managed to get into their own share of trouble, too, especially when they had tried climbing the walls of the castle and were caught more than once.

Victoria and Gabrielle became especially good friends. Victoria was eventually able to unload her disillusioned past and was able to talk bravely about her life and dreams. Gabrielle felt that she had found someone who understood her crazy quest for righteousness and beauty through art, ignoring the cold burden of reality and sanity. In retrospect, they were kind of like Cervantes' Don Quijote and Sancho Panza. Except neither was really Sancho; they were both dreamers like Don Quijote. They were idealists following their dreams.

At the end of her first year in Denmark, Victoria had decided to remain one more year with her father. While there, she had decided to become a contentious runner. She had been running at school and throughout her neighborhood, continually challenging her friends to races, but she began to seriously take up the sport when she met Girt, a high school German soccer player whose team was training in Denmark.

Girt was a sophomore in high school, and Victoria was only in the 8$^{th}$ grade at the time. She had met Girt while canoeing at Bagsværd Lake near her home. The lake had often hosted international rowing, canoeing and kayak competitions, but there were times when one could just rent a canoe and paddle around at leisure. Girt and four of his teammates had been canoeing at the lake one afternoon at the same time that Victoria and Gabrielle had joined her family for a picnic and time out on the lake. Jack and his wife had stayed on the shore with Steven, and Victoria and Gabrielle had taken the canoe out for a while. The girls had spotted the boys in their canoe, so they feigned ignorance about canoeing and they spun their craft around in circles while laughing as loud as they could to attract attention. The four Scandinavian boys had quickly noticed, and they naturally came to their rescue. The problem was that they only spoke German. No Spanish. No

French. Not even a bit of English. Girt had motioned that he was going to jump into the water and come to their rescue. The girls encouraged the lifesaving gesture, and Girt called their bluff by jumping into the lake. He had appeared to be the leader of the group, more outspoken, and certainly the handsomest. He swam valiantly to their canoe and requested permission to come aboard. He hoisted himself into the canoe and took them ashore with his three friends and their canoe in tow. Once on solid ground, they had laughed and gestured and had somehow understood each other by speaking every language they knew hoping that a few words would be internationally understood.

Girt and his friends had managed to ask the girls out on a date that evening. It would be Victoria's first date. His audacity had impressed her, even though she was a bit timid about going on a date with someone she had just met in a country that she barely knew. Jack had granted permission, to her surprise, so the girls left to get ready for their date. Surely she would have to wear some make-up. She had been preparing for this day for a long time; well, for a long time in an eighth grader's mind. Maybe she would even wear stockings. No, no stockings, she had decided. They were going to be going to Tivoli, an amusement park, so a dress was out of the question. She had only brought one dress with her from Puerto Rico the previous year, and it was yellow with green flowers and just a bit too frilly now that she was all grown up. Again, as grown up as an eighth grader could be.

Girt and Victoria had somehow been paired together, and Gabrielle had been paired with his friend. The boys must have discussed the arrangement in advance and had decided who was going to walk around with whom. The group was accompanied by three other members of the soccer team and they had all met at the entrance of Tivoli Gardens at about five o'clock. Victoria and Gabrielle had taken the train to Copenhagen's Central Station since the gardens were only about a block away from the station. Jack had trusted them to go alone and had reminded them that they

CHERYL HOLDEFER

needed to be home by ten o'clock. Times were different back then, and it wasn't unusual for teenagers to ride the trains all around by themselves. The crime rate in Denmark had been extremely low and the trains were very safe.

Tivoli Gardens had originally been a part of Copenhagen's fortifications, and in 1841 it had been converted into an amusement park by King Christian VIII so that he could entertain his subjects. It was a magical and mystical amusement park with hundreds of thousands of gorgeous flowers all around it. It was a wonderful place to take a long stroll through the many rows of flowers in the evenings, because they all lit up with romantic twinkling lights at night. There were often free live concerts in the Concert Hall in the gardens. There were beer gardens that came alive as the night grew late, and there were open air cafés where one could just sit and watch the people stroll by.

There were fireworks at midnight at the park, and Victoria had wished that they could have stayed long enough to see them. It didn't matter, though, because fireworks had already been exploding with passion in her young mind as she held hands for the first time ever with a boy. The two boys with Victoria and Gabrielle hadn't really been interested in the romantic gardens, however. They were happy to bypass them and go directly to the area of the park with the rides. So the two couples rode on as many rides as they could. They had finally come to the roller coaster. Victoria remembered laughing nervously as the coaster pulled itself up the wooden girders and rushed through a tunnel before plummeting downward and spiraling upwards once more. Girt had tried to kiss Victoria in the tunnel, and she had pushed him away at the last minute. No offense had been taken by him, but he did ask her why she hadn't wanted to kiss him. She couldn't really explain and she used the language barrier as an excuse. The fact was that she had just been too nervous and her first impulse had been to push him away. She wished she hadn't. But she got another chance when she accepted a contest challenge for the next day. The girls would go to Alsborg and watch the soccer scrimmage against the Danish team. If Girt's team won, Victoria would owe him a kiss.

Girt's team won. Victoria remembered how he had run over to her on the sidelines and had kissed her passionately on the lips. She had felt his face close to hers and the warm breath on her cheeks. There had been no violent exploration, only lingering softness. Then he held her face in his hands and looked into her eyes. No words, just feelings cascading though their eyes lost in an endless adventure. He had gently touched her lips with his once more, and then he ran back to the team to celebrate with his friends.

That evening after the soccer game the girls had been joined by their friends Hillary and Carole, and Girt and his teammates accompanied them all to dinner in the city near their dormitory, Elers Kollegium, where they had been staying at the University of Copenhagen for the two weeks of soccer camp. They still had another day left in Copenhagen and had asked the girls if they would go with them the next day to the Royal Deer Park, or *Dyrehaven*, since they had heard so much about it. The boys had wanted to find a path they might be able to run on as part of their endurance training for soccer. Their coach had suggested the park since it was only about fifteen minutes from the city.

King Christian V had received the forest as a gift from the State of Denmark in 1650. He had decided to use it as a place for hunting deer and he built a beautiful hunting lodge in the middle called Eremitagen. This was where the group had decided to meet the next day around noon. There were about 2,000 deer in the park, but they shared it with humans who wished to walk, cycle or run through the park during the summer, or even do some skiing in the winter. Victoria gladly shared the park with the deer, she reflected, because she had been anxious to see the person she had hopelessly fallen in love with one more time before he had to return to Germany.

Victoria had been excited yet nervous about the meeting in

Dyrehaven. She had asked Girt if she could join him and his teammates on their run in the park. Gabrielle and their two friends had agreed to wait for the boys at Eremitagen where they'd have food for a picnic when the group had finished their run. Victoria had already been to the park several times, so she knew the trails they were going to run and she was confident about her first running experience with boys.

What had begun as a practice run eventually became a competition for Victoria. Girt and Victoria had started out in the front of the pack with a slow jog. Then Girt stepped up the pace and teasingly smiled back at his opponent. Victoria wondered if she should challenge him and quicken her pace to stay in front with him, or if she should be girly and take a place in the middle of the pack or in the rear. The challenge was too inviting, she had decided. She breezed past the other soccer players on the path and joined Girt in the front. Girt had laughed and motioned that they should race to the end. She nodded with enthusiasm and sprinted out ahead of him. She knew the path well. Only two more kilometers to the end. She persevered and quickened her pace as Girt came up quickly from behind. Her breathing had become labored. The acceleration had been too fast, she realized. But she wasn't going to back down. The playful race became a contest of endurance and soon Girt and Victoria had pulled out far ahead of the pack. He ran seemingly effortlessly beside her as she felt her chest burning and she began gasping for air. Her mouth was dry. She saw the hill coming, lowered her head, leaned forward and quickened her pace. But Girt was right beside her. "*No!*" he shouted at her. At first Victoria hadn't understood, but then she saw him motion to his chest to indicate that she should straighten up, pull her chin up, and pump her arms so that her fists approached her nose. She maintained the pace and could feel her arms pull her up the hill. She had steadied her breathing and had focused straight ahead. By keeping her back straight, she found she had been able to lift her knees higher and push off on her toes to climb the hills.

By keeping her head up she had been able to breathe deeper and steadier. Girt had pulled ahead of her a bit and she saw that his running style changed with the terrain. She imitated him. At the end of the path near the hunting lodge Girt had slowed down to let Victoria win. She had laughed and pushed him ahead of her. She was definitely in love.

On that day, however, Victoria had learned another valuable lesson, not in love, but about running. She had learned that there were some very minute details in running form, just the slightest changes, that could make considerable differences in speed and endurance.

Later in the evening Victoria had said good-bye once more to Girt. This was their last evening in Denmark, and Victoria regretted that she had met Girt at the end of the team's trip instead of at the beginning. Victoria and Girt parted sadly that evening knowing that a future relationship would hopelessly disintegrate because of the language barrier and the distance. They wouldn't even be able to write letters, really. She had been so young then. But love didn't understand age. She hadn't regretted the time spent with Girt even knowing that he would be gone forever. Her father Jack had once told her that she should live for the moment, creating treasured memories for tomorrow from those moments lived today.

# CHAPTER FIVE

"Jennifer! It's Aunt Rina! Are you home, sweetie?"

"She's upstairs, Rina. They just finished the softball game and she's taking a shower." Victoria smiled as she walked to the foyer to greet and hug her sister. Rina always barged into the house without knocking, but Victoria was quite alright with that. She always enjoyed Rina's visits.

"Good, I want to talk to you before Jennifer comes downstairs."

*Here it comes*, thought Victoria.

"Listen, I'm going to have some of Rob's friends over for a little dinner later this evening and I'd like you to come," her sister said.

"Rina, you're trying to set me up with a date again, aren't you?"

"Most certainly *not*! I just thought that Christopher and Jennifer probably had plans on a Saturday night and you would be all alone and…"

"Well first of all, Chris isn't going anywhere because he's typing that term paper for college. He is only here for the weekend. And I have a stack of term papers to grade this weekend for my own students." Victoria told a little white lie, but those lies were sometimes necessary when her dear sister was trying to set her up with another boring date.

"Oh no you don't! I'm not falling for the *grading papers* lie! Come on, Vicky, you have been divorced for five years now and I've hardly ever seen you go out on a date. You just work and take care of the kids. What are you waiting for?"

"It's only been three years, Rina."

"Okay, so you've been separated for two years and divorced

for three. Semantics. You need to go out and have some fun."

"Are you two fighting again?" asked Jennifer as she entered the room. "You know mom is going to win, Aunt Rina. Older sisters *always* win!" Jennifer laughed as she walked towards the kitchen and opened the refrigerator door.

"Maybe we should talk at another time," whispered Rina.

"I can hear you!" chimed in Jennifer. "Aunt Rina, I'm graduating from high school in two months. I think I'm old enough to hear this conversation. And I agree, mom, you should get out more. You know, like hang out at the grocery store or Laundromat to see what happens. Maybe a rich handsome man will come in to do some laundry or something, and he'll scoop you off your feet and take you to Burger Palace in his white Mercedes."

"In his white *Jaguar*," Victoria reciprocated.

"Okay, you two! Cut it out! I know when I've been defeated by my own family!" Rina laughed and kissed her niece on the head as Jennifer bit into an apple she found in a bowl on the kitchen counter.

"Anyway," Rina persevered, "the offer still stands, Vicky. No match-making. I promise it's just a dinner," she said with a sly smile. "Okay, Jennifer, let's get going to the mall to look for your prom dress."

"Okay. See you later mom!" Jennifer blew her mom a kiss as she grabbed her purse off a chair.

A few minutes later they pulled out of the driveway and Rina honked the horn of the car as she rounded the corner out of the cul-de-sac.

Victoria sat on the sofa after they left, with her glass of wine in hand, and she thought about her sister Rina and how she wished her sister had been able to have a child of her own. Not that she minded loaning Jennifer to her. She thought about how Rina had moved to the States from Puerto Rico way back when to attend school on the mainland with her scholarship from Moore College of Art. But then Rina had gotten pregnant at the age of 20, quit college and got married, and she lost the baby four months later. Her husband had left her shortly thereafter. Good riddance, Victoria thought. He was a jerk. But Rina was not a quitter. She had gone back to school and thrown herself into marketing design and advertising. She was brilliant. A large advertising firm in Washington D.C. had recruited her after graduation, and after settling in, she had sent for her mother Rebecca to come and live with her in a condominium near Georgetown.

Victoria thought back to when her mom had stayed in Puerto Rico when she had gone off to Denmark to live with her father for those two years. Rebecca had wanted to stay on the island so that Rina could have some continuity in her life while her only sister was gone. When Victoria returned to Puerto Rico, Rebecca had already decided to stay there indefinitely rather than return to the States. The girls would then be able to attend high school on the island and be with their friends in the only place that they knew as their home. There was no sense uprooting them again and risking assimilation problems with a new culture. Rebecca had been immersed in life with a promotion at the *San Juan Star* and was making a decent living. She had some friends that she attended concerts and art shows with, and she knew that Rina was thriving at school and loving her friends and her little dog Benji. Besides, she didn't think Benji could make the trip to the States without having a fit on the airplane. So Rebecca had changed her mind and had decided to stay on the island, at least until both of the girls had graduated from high school. The cost of living was much lower on the island than in the continental United States, after all.

Victoria and Rina had never liked the idea of leaving Rebecca in Puerto Rico alone once they had moved away from home to attend college on the mainland. It took some convincing to bring her back to the States, but they managed to do so after they had graduated from college and were making some good salaries. Rebecca had moved in with Rina in Washington D.C. at that point, and several years after working in a firm near the Capitol, Rina had moved to Maryland and opened an agency of her own in Baltimore. They only lived about half an hour away from Victoria. It was amazing how they had all lived in so many different countries and yet they had all ended up in the same place!

Although she was quite a successful businesswoman, Rina had never had too much success with long-term relationships. Men appeared to be threatened by her competitive edge and work ethic. She hid her sensitivity well, and whenever a man would get too close, she would unconsciously push him away. But one day this wonderful man walked into her life, and she forgot to push him away.

Their relationship had started years ago when Roberto Ayala had been patiently sitting in the waiting room of Rina's office for nearly half an hour. He was a divorce lawyer and was there to represent his client, one Mrs. Irene Velasco, against her husband, Mr. R. Velasco. What Rob did not realize was that Mr. R. Velasco's office was actually on the fifth floor, and that this was the seventh floor, the office of Ms. *Rina* Velasco. He had grown impatient waiting and had finally approached Rina's secretary, who in turn interrupted Rina to tell her this lawyer was waiting for some appointment that was not on the calendar. Rina came out into the lobby to apologize to the gentleman and explain the confusion between the two Velasco's. It happened all the time, she had said. Twenty minutes later, Rob Ayala was headed down in the elevator to the fifth floor for his appointment holding Rina's business card in his hand. Three months later, the two got married in a small ceremony in the countryside with family and a few friends. Rob was a little older than Rina and had been married once already. He had two older sons in college, so they had decided in advance not to have any more children. Rina didn't care, because this was the man with whom she wanted to spend the rest of her life. So Rina spoiled her niece Jennifer whenever she was around, and Victoria was happy to loan her daughter out whenever Rina had an adventure in mind. As long as she didn't take her for a tattoo or piercing.

Victoria sat there smiling as she started thinking about the excuses she would make to get out of her sister's dinner party where she would surely be set up with some business friend of Rob's that just *happened* to drop in.

# CHAPTER SIX

"*Allo,* Victoria?" came the faraway yet familiar voice on the other end of the phone. "It's me, Gabrielle!"

"*Thank goodness!*" Victoria responded. "I tried calling you at work yesterday, but I didn't have much luck with all those numbers, and then having to bungle my way through French with the long-distance operator was just too much. I'm afraid my French is rusty these days. Ha! Don't you *ever* answer your cell phone?"

"You know I hate cell phones! Someone is always trying to call me and I just don't have the time!" her friend replied with a laugh.

"Okay, so when are you coming to the East Coast for your business trip? Jennifer was really hoping you could come before her prom so you could see her all dressed up."

"I will be in New York in two weeks, and then on to Maryland to visit with you right after that! Good enough?"

"Yes, good. That *is* good news," Victoria said with some hesitation in her voice.

"Vicky, is something going on? I mean, other than Jennifer's prom?" Gabrielle had picked up on her friend's tone. "*Tell me!* Don't make me wait! You know how I hate to wait when you have something important to tell me!"

"Nothing," lied Victoria, "nothing at all. I just knew that you were scheduled to come in sometime soon, so I thought I'd get the dates to put on my calendar."

"What a liar! You think I don't know you after all of these years?" Gabrielle admonished her friend. "*Alors*, I will wait if I must. But we will talk when I get there, *d'accord*?"

"Of course," Victoria agreed, "we'll talk."

Victoria had kept the secret of her affair with Dan Cole to herself for two years, so she could certainly wait a few more weeks to share it with Gabrielle in person instead of getting into it on the phone. She had to sort through her thoughts first anyway. She felt like she was ready to talk to someone about it, though, and Gabrielle was the most logical person. She hoped her friend wouldn't be mad at her for not revealing her secret relationship several years ago when she had visited her in France.

Jennifer's discovery of her mom's short story the previous day had stirred up feelings Victoria had subconsciously been trying to repress for almost two years. She had thought that with time, she would just forget about Dan. After all, women and men have relationships and break-ups all the time, and they just forget about them and move on to the next person, don't they? So maybe talking about the whole thing would bring some finality to the affair, she thought, and then she would move on too.

The word *affair* wasn't really the correct word to use in describing the relationship with Dan, she decided. It wasn't as if she had cheated on a husband to have an extramarital affair. She wasn't married at the time. She and the kids' father, Tom, had split up before she had even met Dan. So there was no reason to feel guilt.

Victoria trusted the Gabrielle would not judge her as she recounted the events that led to this whatever-you-call-it relationship. She knew her friend would be a good listener, too, and maybe even offer some perspective that eluded her to this day.

The relationship with Dan had ended poorly, and she just couldn't sort out her feelings. She had this lingering sense of, what, *guilt*? No, that wasn't it. *Humiliation*? Maybe *deception*? After all, she had caught Dan kissing another woman. Wasn't that justification for her leaving him? *What had he been thinking?* And yet, she couldn't help wondering if maybe she had driven him away somehow without even knowing. She really thought that he had been the one, the one that she had been waiting for. The one that would give meaning to her life. What had happened?

"Mom?" interrupted Christopher, walking into the kitchen. Victoria was flustered and started washing the dishes to get her mind off of her thoughts.

"Here's a letter for Jennifer from the University of Virginia and I think this is the one you two have been waiting for," said Chris. He waited for a moment, and after not getting a response, "Are you okay, mom?"

"What? Oh, yes, I'm okay, honey. I was just on the phone with Gabi and I was trying to remember the dates she gave me for her visit in a couple of weeks."

"Great! I hope she gets here in time for the graduations!" he exclaimed. "Well, I have to leave soon because I have a four-hour drive back to the college." He went to the kitchen and placed the envelope from the university on the counter.

"Okay," she responded. "Do you need anything before you go back, sweetie? Money? Did you get your laundry from downstairs? Here, at least let me get together some snacks for your drive."

Victoria rushed to the pantry to see what she could find for his trip. Chris didn't want to deny his mother this simple pleasure because he knew it was her nature to shelter and protect her children no matter how old they were! He knew that she also carried around some undeserved guilt from the divorce from his father five years ago, so she tended to overcompensate with her children by trying to provide for every need whether they needed anything or not.

Christopher loved his mother dearly and admired her accomplishments immensely. His mom was an excellent English professor, a strong athlete, and a very dedicated mother. She had never let him down as a kid. She had attended almost all of his soccer and baseball games, the little parties at school, the doctors' appointments, the science fairs, and she had driven him to basketball practices, to the library, to friends' birthday parties, and to the movies. She had never complained, not even when she had to drive him to three events on one day!

Now it seemed so long ago since he had been in high school, Christopher thought. Once again this year he would be graduating and stepping into the next phase of his life. He was looking forward to it. He already had a plan. He wanted to open a store for athletic equipment and clothing, and he already had the financial backing he needed and the business degree to go with it. He had begun to build his clientele with the athletic directors at the local schools, and he had a few sports clubs interested as well. He loved sports, and he loved business, so he thought he'd combine both and see where it took him.

Christopher had been quite an athlete, but he had never been as determined as his sister and his mom had been, he reflected. Both of them had boxes of medals and trophies they modestly stored away in the basement. As runners, they were both driven by some inexplicable desire to pound their feet along endless miles of undetermined and sometimes unchartered terrain until they had pushed their legs beyond unparalleled pain. He certainly admired the determination in his little sister and his mother. He had not aspired to become an elite athlete himself; he was more drawn to the business aspect of the sport. At one point he had considered sports medicine or sports news casting, but he knew he possessed his father's draw to finance, the exchange of goods, bartering and hustling, investing, divesting, persuading and attainment. He had begun studying anatomy and physiology in college and had taken courses to be a physical therapist, but then he took a random accounting class at the end of his sophomore year and ended up switching to a business degree in his junior year.

"Here you go, sweetie," said Victoria as she handed him a bag of cookies and chips and fruit and stood on her toes to kiss him on the cheek. "So we won't see you until graduation in May, right?" "Don't worry, mom, it's only two months away! I'll call as usual, okay?" He hugged her and went to pick up his bags at the front door. "Oh, don't forget the letter on the counter for Jen from UVA. Tell me what happens when Jen opens it, okay?" "Okay! I love you! Drive safely!" Victoria stood by the door as she always did and watched his car drive away until it was no longer visible.

Victoria went over to the kitchen counter and picked up the letter from the University of Virginia. It was addressed to her, not Jennifer. Her daughter had already received confirmation of her acceptance into UVA. What she and Jennifer had been waiting for now was the response to the application for a scholarship either through athletics or academics. Victoria opened the letter, and as she carefully read the words her eyes swelled with tears. "*She got it!*" she whispered to herself.

# CHAPTER SEVEN

Victoria thought back to when she had received her own acceptance letter and scholarship to The University of Virginia when she had graduated from high school. She had never considered herself to be a particularly bright student, although she probably had been somewhat, and she would certainly never have figured that an institution like UVA would have taken a chance on some unknown kid from Puerto Rico. And now her daughter was following in her footsteps and going to her *alma mater*!

Victoria held her daughter's scholarship letter in her hands and thought about how she had worked hard to get her own invitation to attend UVA years ago. She remembered thinking that her application had to have something spectacular on it; something that would dazzle the Board somehow. Maybe if she tried to run the length of the island, almost 100 miles, she could show her special talent for distance running. Then maybe the track coach at UVA would take notice and talk to the Admissions Board about inviting her to attend their institution with a full scholarship. Women weren't being offered athletic scholarships for cross country running at that time, but Victoria recalled thinking that she was different; that someone would surely be impressed. She had needed the money, or there would be no college. So she would just run and show them. *It could be done*, she had thought as a determined young teenager. If UVA didn't pick her up, then maybe some other college would.

Victoria recalled how she had decided to start training in the early spring of her junior year of high school so that she would be ready to run in the fall right as she was applying to colleges. She had picked UVA as her first choice from a catalog she had found on the counter in her English class at *Academia San José*. She had known nothing about the college, nothing about Virginia, but she had read about a coach at the college that had trained one of the top male runners several years past. The runner had continued on to run in the Olympics after graduating from the college. Victoria wanted to run in the Olympics. Only women didn't run in the Olympics. She would change that someday. In order to run the distance of 100 miles, she had figured that seven months of training would be enough. And surely her high school would allow her to take off a few days from the fall term to do the run, wouldn't they?

Victoria had been running since she had attended school in Denmark in the 7$^{th}$ and 8$^{th}$ grades. When she returned to Puerto Rico to live with her mother and her sister Rina, she had continued to run throughout her high school years. But *Academia San José*, the Catholic high school for girls that she had attended in Villa Caparra, didn't have a team. Actually, they didn't even have a gym or equipment or a coach that could help her. But Victoria hadn't needed a team or coach or equipment. There were plenty of streets to run on and plenty of palm trees to shield her from the heat as she ran.

During the spring of her junior year, Victoria had gradually begun increasing her mileage. She had decided that it would take her about five days to cover the 100-mile distance if she ran about twenty miles per day. Of course, that would be as the crow flies. She'd have to have some assistance by car for the places where the roads ended or the highways had been blocked by mountains.

In those days, there hadn't been much literature on training for long distances for women. Not much for her to refer to when she had been trying to set up her own running plan. Although men had been racing marathons since the late 1800's, women were unheard of in long distance racing, or even short distance racing. Roberta Gibb was the first woman to run the full Boston Marathon in 1966, and even at that, she had had to hide in the bushes near the start until the race began. Roberta had submitted an application to run, but it had been returned to her with a note saying that women were not physically capable of running a marathon. Well, she did. She finished with an unofficial time of 3:21:25. In 1967 Katherine Switzer had identified herself as K. V. Switzer on the racing application, so she had been issued a bib number. She had been only twenty years old. The Boston Athletic Association figured out that she was a girl when she was about two miles into the race, and they tried unsuccessfully to remove her from the race. The race director and an official for the BAA had actually come out into the race and tried to grab her number and take her out of the race, but one of the male friends who was running with her body-blocked him and sent the official sprawling onto the road. She resumed the race surrounded by fellow teammates from Syracuse University who continued to fend off the officials with their bodies. Women were finally permitted to participate in marathons in the fall of 1971. It was about time. In 1972 eight women started the Boston Marathon, and all eight finished, with Nina Kuscsik becoming the first official champion. Grete Waitz won her first New York City Marathon in 1978 and had had to ask the race director for $20 for cab fare since there had been no compensation for winning in those days. Then in 1981 Lorraine Moller accepted money for the *Cascade Run-off* 15-kilometer road race in Portland, and that had been the first time women could get prize money without being disqualified.

It took longer, however, for the Olympics to catch up with women in marathons. The Executive Board finally approved the women's marathon race in 1981, Victoria remembered, and women participated in their first marathon of the Olympics on August 5, 1984, in Los Angeles. The American Joan Benoit pulled ahead of the pack just fourteen minutes into the race, and she led the whole distance to finish with a time of 2:24:52, almost two minutes ahead of her competitor. Victoria had dreamed of being one of the first women to run in the Olympics alongside of Joan Benoit.

Victoria remembered how she had figured out her own training plan to accomplish her feat of running the 100 miles to impress the trustees of UVA. She had started with a long run every Saturday of five miles and had added one mile to that every week. On the other days she did shorter runs. At first she had run every day. After three weeks she realized that she had been overdoing it and stressing her body. She had never given it time to rebuild and get stronger. So she experimented varying the lengths of her runs, always keeping that one long run on the weekend as she increased distance, and taking off one day to rest. Eventually she had decided to take off two days, not consecutive, but on one of those days she would swim instead of run. It hadn't cost her anything to go to the beach in Puerto Rico, and water was everywhere! Shark season was in November, so she hadn't been too worried. But Victoria had known nothing about speed training, surging, fartlek or interval workouts, and it hadn't mattered much anyway, because she wasn't going to be competing against anyone, only herself. Her goal was simply to cover the distance. She had learned a lot about endurance training: how to eat, what made her sick, how to drink water before, during, and after her runs, and how to pop her blisters by threading them and leaving the thread in so that they couldn't fill up with liquid again the next day. Victoria reminisced about how she had been so committed to getting into college. She had carefully selected and wrote to six colleges in addition to UVA. When she sent in the applications, she had attached a letter explaining her goal to run across the island in hopes that one of the colleges would want to give her an athletic scholarship.

It was October first nearing seven o'clock in the morning when Victoria had begun her *Run for a Scholarship*, as she had called it. She had decided to begin early so that she could stay ahead of some of the hot temperatures that would surely emerge later in the day. Word traveled fast, and there had been close to thirty people at the starting line to cheer her on her journey. A couple of her classmates from high school had been there with

Sister Mary Joseph, her English teacher, and they had all said a little prayer with her. One of the reporters from the *San Juan Star* was there at Rebecca's request, although he had been skeptical about this story amounting to much. Two coaches from universities to which Victoria had written had actually sent a local informant to watch her. There weren't any scouts in those days; just informants. She hadn't seen anyone from the University of Virginia, however. Again, it hadn't mattered, because she knew she was going to go to college somewhere, and someone would surely give her a scholarship. They just had to.

Victoria had decided to begin her trek on the south western seaboard of the island in a small town called Boquerón. On the way to her starting point, she recollected, the engine of her mom's car had caught on fire and some nice man took off his shirt, put out the fire, and then convinced a taxi driver to drive them the rest of the distance to where she would begin her venture. The cab driver had been curious and had been glad to oblige. Victoria had decided that her starting point would be at a hotel called *La Parguera* at the bottom of a steep hill. She would try to run twenty one and a half miles that first day and had planned to finish the afternoon in Guánica. Rebecca and a few friends were to follow by car with water and anything else Victoria had needed. Since the car had broken down, however, Plan B was to have the reporter from the *Star* drive Rebecca around.

Victoria remembered that on the first day that she had run, she had finished in about five hours and fifty minutes. She had been exhausted, but very proud of her time. By the end of the run, her hair had been matted down from the sweat and she looked awful, but she had been healthy and in good spirits. The reporter hadn't seen anything extraordinary, so he was ready to leave, but as a colleague and friend to Rebecca, he had decided to stay another day. Small hotels had given Victoria and her family a few rooms at reduced rates. Her high school, *Academia San José*, had contributed money for some food. Victoria had just been grateful for the large spaghetti dinner that night and the long hours of sleep that followed after soaking her feet!

The second day had not been bad either. It rained, which cooled down the streets considerably. It had been a good distracter for her and she had kept strong. She wore elastic knee braces and paid attention to the placement of her feet so as not to injure her knees. She finished her nineteen miles to Ponce in about six hours. Longer than the previous day with less distance, she had thought, but the key was to stay healthy. The reporter from the *Star* took a picture of her at that point, and sent in a two-paragraph story for the next day. The story had appeared on the last page of the newspaper.

On the third day, Victoria had woken up with stomach cramps. She must have eaten something she shouldn't have, she had decided, but surely it would pass. It didn't. Halfway through her run that day, it let loose and ran down her legs. She had been so embarrassed, she recalled. Her mother and members of Antonio's family who were accompanying Rebecca on the trip that day had urged her to stop for the day, but she hadn't, because it wasn't in her plan. She knew the delay would just extend the hours for the following day. She had decided to just try walking some of the distance and then play it by ear. She got cleaned up at a nearby town, changed clothes, and set out to finish her miles for the day. When she had arrived at her checkpoint in Salinas that afternoon, she had been severely dehydrated and was taken to the hospital and given some saline solution. Rebecca had folded her daughter's clothes in the hospital room as she had waited for her to return from the examining room, and she had found a small picture of Esperanza pinned to the lining inside of Victoria's running shorts. She had held the picture and cried, and then quietly pinned the picture back to the shorts.

Victoria had returned to the road for her fourth day, defying all speculation. She was physically weak, but mentally strong. She had decided not to worry about her time anymore, just her goal to get through Guayama to the other side of Patillas. Two of her small toenails had already turned purple. Her arms felt like lead. She had been losing too much weight. *One more day*, she had prayed, *just one more day*. By the end of that day, another informant had shown up from Penn State University and interviewed her for a position at their college. The University of Puerto Rico had offered her a free ride, and she was grateful to them for supporting her during the entire race, because Puerto Rico was her home.

Then came the final day of her journey. Victoria had been barely able walk. Rebecca had been pleading with her daughter to end the runs, but she knew that this was something Victoria had needed to do for herself to prove her worth. The *San Juan Star* reporter had called in a camera crew and *Radio Mundo* was there as well. This was news. A *girl* was actually running one hundred miles? Unheard of! A caravan of cars had followed her to Yabucoa, and aficionados had lined the roads and had joined her for stretches of the run. She hadn't spoken to anyone, but she had tried valiantly to smile every now and then. She had just kept her focus on the road. Her gaze had been intent. People had clapped as she passed by, and a little girl not more than eight years old had sprinted out into the street and had run with her for about a mile. The girl's name was *Juanita*, Jennifer in English. The little brown girl had told her how much she had admired her and how she had wanted to be just like her when she grew up.

The last five miles had been horrendous. Victoria had battled to simply remain conscious and aware of her surroundings. She had tripped over her own feet and fallen down twice. "Don't touch me!" she had exclaimed to someone trying to help her up. Her eyes had become glazed. She had barely comprehended what she was doing. People sprayed her with water. She had just known some-how that she was supposed to keep running. She was grinding her teeth. She remembered that her feet and legs had been numb beyond pain. Rebecca had been crying for the last seven miles of the event, knowing in her heart that only an irresponsible parent could allow this to continue. But Victoria had explained to her mom that morning that it wasn't about college anymore, it was about who she was as a person. It *defined* her.

By the time Victoria had reached her last mile, there were hundreds of well-wishers, seasoned athletes, and aspiring racers running alongside her to protect her. The media was there to cover the story. When she arrived at her last checkpoint, Victoria remembered painfully, she had collapsed. She was whisked away to the hospital in a waiting ambulance where she spent two nights and three days recovering enough to go home. People had sent cards and flowers to the hospital, and she had been surrounded by fluffy stuffed animals and presents from her friends. Companies had been calling her about interviews, and *Coca Cola* had wanted to talk to her about an endorsement. On her third day in the hospital, as she had prepared her belongings to go home, a tall thin man entered her room.

"How are you feeling?" he had asked.

"Fine" she had responded.

"I am going to recommend you for acceptance to The University of Virginia with a full scholarship and a position on my cross country team. But don't ever do this again."

He had walked slowly to the door and then turned before leaving. "By the way," he had said, "don't accept any endorsements."

Seven days later, Victoria had signed the papers to attend the University of Virginia with a full scholarship. It had been a great gift, and a wise decision.

# CHAPTER EIGHT

"Aunt Gabrielle! Over here!" Jennifer yelled as she raced towards the passengers arriving at Gate 12 at Dulles Airport.

Gabrielle walked as fast as she could in her spiked heels, with her soft brown pixie-haircut bouncing and her green eyes shining with excitement. They hugged and laughed and interrupted each other with quick questions and answers attempting to fill in the gaps since her last visit three years ago.

"Where is your dear mother?!" asked Gabrielle.

"She's outside in the car. We were late getting here because of my softball practice, so I just jumped out of the car when we got to the airport." Jennifer pulled Gabrielle's hand and held onto one of the suitcases with the other as they darted out to the curb where Victoria was waiting in the car.

"Wait 'til I tell you all about my letter from UVA!" exclaimed Jennifer as they hopped into the car.

After dinner that night, Victoria and Gabrielle sat on the deck with a second glass of wine satisfied that they had sufficiently caught up with each others' hectic life stories for the past two years. Jennifer had gone upstairs to study for her impending final exams. The spring term was winding down quickly.

"Confession time, Vicky," her friend said leaning forward.

"What are you talking about?" responded Victoria.

"Why did you call me out of the blue three weeks ago?" asked her friend.

"I missed you! And I knew your visit was coming up soon!"

"I'm not buying it, Vicky. Something is going on, and I want to know about it."

"Okay," sighed Victoria. She trusted Gabrielle implicitly, so that was not the issue. Victoria was just afraid that if she heard herself talk about what was on her mind, she would have to relive the sadness and confusion of the broken relationship with Dan. And it hurt. Still.

"Okay," Victoria said again. "It goes back five years ago, right after separating from Tom. Awkward timing, I guess, and completely unexpected."

"I have nowhere to go, so start from the beginning."

Victoria went back to her memories of five years prior when she had just finished training for a race in hopes of qualifying for the Olympic marathon trials. She had known she could qualify, even though she had been an unknown runner at the time. She had written a letter to her former coach at UVA to ask for his advice, because everyone, including her almost ex-husband, had seemingly opposed her decision to attempt this challenge. The coach had told her to go for it. She had known that she would be one of the oldest contenders, so this would have been her last chance to qualify.

"*Are you crazy?*" her husband, from whom she had already been separated, had asked when she had told him about her plan. He had been convinced that she was going to die and leave him with two children to raise without a mother. He warned that the training would take time away from the children, which it did at times. But she hadn't told him that she had already been training for almost a year right under his nose.

Even her friends in the neighborhood had thought that she was going through an early mid-life crisis. '*Couldn't you just dye your hair or something?*' they had asked. And she did. But it hadn't been enough.

Victoria recounted to her friend Gabrielle about how she had had this wonderful sixteen-year-old son and twelve-year-old daughter, had been married for seventeen years to a successful intelligent senior vice-president of a reputable investment firm, herself recently accepted for a post as associate professor at Johns Hopkins University, and she had felt unhappy in a marriage that she should have worked on instead of trying to qualify for an Olympic marathon. She had asked for a separation only months before telling Tom about the marathon, and he had moved out in hopes that she would see the light and ask him to eventually come back.

As she remembered these past events, Victoria thought about how she had set running aside when her children had been born. The children had been the most wonderful thing that had ever happened to her and Tom, truly, and she hadn't wanted to miss a moment of their lives when she came home each day from work and they came home from school. She had coordinated their schedules so that she would be home as soon as they got home. Running had been out of the question at that time in her life, and she hadn't even missed it. She had known that when the kids got older, they would probably prefer spending time with their own friends, so she knew she would probably take up running again at that point. However, she had never thought about running *competitively* again. Then somewhere along the line, the little Halloween and Valentine's Day parties at school had been replaced with high school sports and dances, and the kids hadn't seemed to need their mom's undivided attention any longer. Tom hadn't needed it either. Victoria was proud of whom her children had become, and she was happy that they had had such wonderful groups of friends and that they had so many different talents. Everyone had been healthy, and everyone had been happy. Except Victoria.

Tom and Victoria had lost sight of their marriage without even realizing it. She knew that she had cared for Christopher and Jennifer's father, but their marital relationship had steered off along the way, and there hadn't been much of a foundation to build on even when going to couples counseling. They hadn't been spending much time together as a couple, and probably hadn't even done that before the children were born. He had always been a workaholic, and she had been just as bad. They had had mutual friends with whom they spent plenty of time, but they had never gone out much just as a couple. They had had similar values and goals, and that was probably what had brought them together in the first place. They had been good partners. He was a decent man, and she knew when she had married him that he would be a great provider and father, faithful and loyal to his family and wife. He didn't gamble and he didn't drink. He had just worked, and so had she. Their days had all looked the same: they came home, she made dinner and he read the newspaper, he washed the dishes as she got the kids' lunches ready for the next day, and then they played with the children until bedtime or watched TV. All the talk at the table had been about work, about the news, about the kids, but never about them. They had been respectful of each other, and kind. Tom was a good man for sure. But something had been missing. Victoria was not naïve enough to think it had been passion, because that lasted for only a few years in a marriage before a couple fit comfortably into their routines and jobs and hobbies precluding each other. *What then?* The relationship had been comfortable. Shouldn't that have been enough? Victoria had not been happy, and yet she had not been able to define the reason. They had been separated and divorced for five years now, and she still couldn't explain it to Gabrielle any better than she had explained it to her five years ago.

Victoria remembered that the worst part of asking for the divorce had been explaining to the children what she hadn't quite understood herself. Tom had screamed at her in anger and had accused her of all kinds of things: maybe she was having an affair, maybe she was a homosexual, or maybe she was confused and needed to find God. It had been worse than running the one hundred miles across the island back in high school. She had thought about Esperanza's death, and Antonio's, and she had known that this loss of the marriage was painful, but it had not been the same as losing a life. There had been no death. The children would still have their father, and they would still have her. They would all recover. Life would go on.

Gabrielle knew all of this, of course, so Victoria started to fill her friend in on the events after the marriage separation five years ago. Although Gabrielle knew Victoria had run the Chicago marathon five years ago and had qualified for the Olympic trials, she listened again to the story knowing that it would lead to whatever had been bothering Victoria these past few years.

Victoria reminded her friend about the race. Her bib number at the Chicago Marathon had been high, number 127, so no one had expected her to be at the head of the pack. She had wanted to finish in two hours and fifty minutes. She had been competing against known winners, experts in their field. She had not been viewed as a serious contender until the seventeenth mile of the race when she broke away and set a one-hundred yard advantage. Victoria had showed no signs of backing off. She finished third at a time of two hours and forty two minutes. She would be headed to the Olympic trials a year and a half later.

Throughout the next year, Victoria recalled, she had restructured her life as a single person and mother. She had spent her days working at the university and training either in the morning or evening when her children were at school or with friends. She would not sacrifice her time with them. They were her priority, not the race. She had determined that at any time, if she had felt that the training was interfering with their lives, she would quit and never look back. But things had worked out, and she had been able to juggle teaching her classes at the university and spending time at her children's sports events.

Victoria met Dan Cole on a Wednesday, and this began the story that she had kept secret even from her friend Gabrielle.

Victoria remembered how she had been standing on the track listening to her trainer Carl lecture her about going too fast on the days of her longer runs.

"You'll burn out! Never recover! Don't you get it? Everyone knows you speed on your interval runs and go easier on the long runs! If you are going to go to the Olympics, you had better listen to what I am telling you!" he had been saying.

"He's right, you know," Dan had said as he walked up behind Carl and Victoria surprising them both.

"Hey, Dan, old buddy! What the hell are you doing all the way down in this area?!" Carl had exclaimed as he and Dan shook hands and embraced.

"Victoria, this is an old high school buddy of mine from way back when a soda pop only cost a nickel and white boys didn't hang with black boys!" Carl was African American, so Dan must have been the *white boy* to which he had been referring.

"We were the best damned sprinters in the whole county, weren't we, Dan?!"

Dan had looked to be about her age, maybe a couple of years older. He was tall and thin with gorgeous brown hair and piercing blue eyes. He had a crooked smile and beautiful straight teeth. Dan had extended his hand to Victoria. She had realized she had been staring, so she quickly shook his hand and looked away. There had been a presence about him that she couldn't explain. His voice had been soft, and yet he had had tremendous confidence and poise.

"Don't mind Carl," Dan had said to Victoria, "soda was never a nickel in my days!" The men had laughed and continued talking for a while and Victoria went back to training on the track.

*This was it*, she had thought to herself as she had run another lap around the track that day. This was what had been missing from her life.

# CHAPTER NINE

"Did you ever see him again?" asked Gabrielle, as she listened intently to her friend's story.

"Yes," she sighed. "He must have gotten my number from Carl."

She continued to tell her friend about the emotion she had felt when she had received that unexpected phone call.

"*Hello?*" the voice had come from the phone. "I'm calling for Victoria Taylor."

"This is she."

"Hello, Victoria. This is Dan Cole. We met yesterday afternoon on the track. I'm Carl's friend."

"Yes, of course!" She couldn't believe it. No, this couldn't have been the same person. But it was. She shouldn't sound too excited, she remembered thinking.

"Carl was telling me that he is working with you to get ready for the Olympic trials next year. He's one of the best, you know."

"Yes, he certainly is! I qualified, so I guess I should give it a shot!" *Act normal*, she had thought. *Act normal. Deep breaths.*

"He mentioned that you are going down hills too fast and suffering from delayed muscle soreness, which is interfering with your training schedule."

"I know. I can't seem to find a comfortable speed between sprinting and braking downhill. So I'm either getting that delayed soreness the next day from going too fast or I'm getting the fatigue in my quadriceps from the braking. I can't seem to find the middle ground no matter how much I listen to Carl." She had felt more controlled. They were on neutral ground. The conversation was safe.

"My book covers that topic. Have you read it?" he had asked unassumingly.

"No. I mean, I'm sorry, but I didn't know you had a book out. So you have a book out?" *What an idiotic thing to say,* she had thought. *Stop bumbling!*

Dan had only laughed.

"Listen," he ventured, "I can meet you out on the track sometime this weekend and give you some pointers if you'd like. Sometimes another perspective helps."

"That would be great! Yes, I could definitely use some pointers." *That's all*, she had thought. *Just some pointers.* There was nothing to this.

"Okay, Friday then. Three o'clock?"

"Yes. No! I forgot, but I'm not on the track on Friday. I have to do the Sligo Creek run. Can you meet on Saturday?" She had held her breath. *Please say yes!*

"Sure. What time?"

"Is eight too early?"

"Eight it is! I'll see you there, Victoria. Nice talking to you."

"Bye!" she had said and hung up the phone.

She told Gabrielle that she remembered staring at the phone for several minutes when the conversation was over. Then she had looked across the room and seen Jennifer at a table intently doing her homework. Jennifer hadn't heard her mother's conversation with Dan, but Victoria had been nervous all the same. She remembered going over and hugging her daughter.

"Well then, did he meet you on the track as he said?" asked Gabrielle.

"Yes."

Victoria poured another glass of wine before recounting the events that led to their first meeting alone.

# CHAPTER TEN

"Okay," Dan had said, "you need to start training downhill twice a week on your easy running days after you've warmed up for about a mile. You want a hill that doesn't have much of a slope and has a stretch of flat ground at the bottom. Start out with two or three 400-meter repeats and add one or two a week. Make sure you're running back up the hill slowly. Don't bound or over stride and don't slap your feet on the ground as you come down. Keep your stride somewhat short at first and increase your turnover. Lengthen your stride slowly, as long as you still feel in control. No leaning, and no slapping, okay?"

"What happens at the bottom of the hill?" Victoria had asked.

"Continue your stride rate just a bit, about fifteen seconds, and then slow your turnover."

"Let's try it," she had said. "There's a perfect slope behind the middle school about a mile from here, so we can run the mile as a warm-up."

"You're on!"

At the end of the practice that day, they had stood around making small talk not knowing how to leave this. He wasn't her coach; Carl was, so he couldn't just hang around every day. But she had known that he wasn't ready to give her up, either.

"I'd like to see you again," he had said. As simple as that.

"I would like that," she had responded.

"I have to go out on business to New Orleans next week, but I'll call when I get back."

"Sure." She had tried to act nonchalant about what he had just said.

"Victoria--"

"Yes?"

"Uhm, well … I noticed that you are resting too long between your warm-up and your run. You shouldn't warm-up and then stand around for awhile before your run. No more than thirty seconds, okay?" She knew that this really wasn't what he had wanted to say. It was just hard saying good-bye.

"I know," she had said, "the oxygen to the leg muscles. I don't normally do that."

"Okay, I'll see you in a week." He had smiled and walked away.

"One week is definitely more than seven days!" Victoria laughed as she got to this part of her story.

"But at the end of the week," she continued recounting to Gabrielle, "Dan called just as he had promised. We agreed to go to a running clinic in Alexandria the evening before the Key Bridge half-marathon. I thought that going to a clinic would be safe. It was legitimate and logical."

Victoria explained how he had met her at a coffee shop and they had driven together to the running clinic. The scheduled speaker had been held up in Pennsylvania, so he had been replaced by a substitute runner; a decent runner, but not a champion.

"Do you really want to stay for this?" he had asked.

They had decided to leave the clinic and go to Old Town Alexandria for dinner. They had parked the car and walked along King Street looking for some restaurant that had brass railings that led up to a bar with a grand piano in the room.

"Dan had heard about the restaurant," Victoria explained to Gabrielle, "but he hadn't been able to recall the name."

Victoria was quiet for a moment while she remembered the feeling of being with Dan on that evening. All the shops along the street had been softly lit, their warmth inviting, and the bright colored objects within had been enticing. As they walked along the main street trying awkwardly to engage in conversation, she remembered how all of a sudden Dan had grabbed her hand and pulled her into a doorway. He had brought her close to his chest and had looked into her eyes. The night air was warm, she remembered, but she had been trembling. Then she recalled how he bent down and brushed his lips against hers. *I'm sorry,* he had said. She had said nothing. She remembered the tenderness as he had drawn her closer and had held her head against his chest for a long time. He had kissed her head.

"And so, did you find the restaurant?" Gabrielle interrupted her friend's thoughts.

"Oh. Well, we were walking along looking for this restaurant and a man opened the door behind where we were leaning and he came out followed by a very classy woman. It reminded me of those old movies you see of rich people in the 50's. He was talking to her about some painting, a Gauguin, I think, that he felt would go well in their front room because it had a bunch of bright yellows and greens. Then I realized Dan and I had been standing in the doorway of a small art gallery. He wanted to go in and look. He asked if I liked art, and I remember thinking to myself *if only Gabi could be here now!*"

"This is true! I probably would have loved being there at that moment to show off my expertise in front of your handsome new man!" They both laughed. Victoria knew her friend certainly would have made an impression on him. Gabrielle had gone back to France after graduating from high school in Denmark and had studied art at the Sorbonne. She had become an expert in her own right.

Victoria continued to explain that the clerk in the gallery had been very attentive, perhaps because she and Dan had both been nicely dressed. Victoria had chosen a silk lilac long-sleeved shirt to wear with her cream slacks. Dan had worn khakis and a black shirt. It had been curious to her, however, that he had worn a brown leather jacket in those warm temperatures. But then it did tend to get chilly in the evenings down by the water at the end of King Street near the Torpedo Factory in Old Town.

"Are you looking for something in particular?" the clerk in the gallery had asked.

"Actually, I'm moving shortly and I'll need to decorate some new rooms," Dan had responded. He had been separated from his wife for almost two years, and he had been building his own house while living in an apartment.

"Look!" Victoria had exclaimed as she had rushed over to the lithographs on the far wall. "It's an original lithograph signed by Michel Delacroix! I know this one. *L'Aèroplane*, right?" she had asked the attendant.

"Would you and your husband like me to take it down for closer inspection? This is a hand-pulled original limited edition lithograph of three hundred artists' proofs." Victoria had realized that the clerk thought they were married.

"No, thank you. We haven't moved yet," Dan had replied, "so I don't want to purchase anything in haste." He took Victoria's hand and walked out the door.

After leaving the gallery, Victoria recalled, he hadn't let go of her hand. Following a few awkward moments of silence, they both had burst out laughing.

"Okay, we're still looking for the restaurant with large glass windows and a shiny spiraling brass staircase," he had smiled.

"There!" exclaimed Victoria as she had pointed across the street.

It had been more beautiful than any restaurant she had ever seen. Or maybe it had been Dan's warmth that had illuminated the room and gave it such a sense of undiscovered charm. Delicate china, sparkling silverware and freshly cut flowers had garnered the tables covered with white linen cloths. Unframed oil paintings likened to Monet's delicate gardens had decorated the white stucco walls. A single crystal chandelier had hung from a dark wooden beam high above their heads. It had been the polished brass banister that had initially allured them. She remembered that they could hear the light jazz coming from the room above.

They had held hands at the table as they began the inquiry into each others' lives. Victoria remembered telling him about her childhood in Puerto Rico and Denmark as Dan had quietly listened. Then he had begun to unfold his own story, and Victoria had been captivated. She had listened intensely to every word. Dan's story had been filled with complexities, and Victoria had yearned to know him completely.

Victoria shared with Gabrielle that Dan had been only fifteen years old when his father left the home. Dan took on the role that his father had chosen to relinquish so that he could protect the four younger siblings that his dad had left behind. He believed that his father had never much cared for him anyway, because he had never gone to any of his sporting events like the other dads did. He had never tucked him in bed at night as a child nor read him a story nor thrown him a ball. His father had never commended him for his good grades. Dan recounted one time when his mother had taped a test paper on the refrigerator that Dan was particularly proud of; his father had ripped it off the door saying that a B was not good enough. Dan remembered snatching the paper off the floor where his father had thrown it and ripping it into hundreds of small pieces. He felt like he had never been the child his father had wanted him to be. Dan told Victoria about the night that his father left for good. It had been raining outside. Dan had just finished competing at an indoor track meet for his school during his sophomore year. He had been scheduled to compete in three events at the meet, but at the last minute, the coach told him to fill in on a relay team because the athlete he was replacing had been injured in a long jump event. During the relay, his teammate approached him on the track for a blind pass of the baton, and an athlete on the opposing team accidentally tripped him. Dan fell to the ground, and by the end of the relay, he could barely walk. But he continued to compete in the remaining events he had trained for, because he feared his father calling him a quitter. Dan had been a champion runner on his team, and he knew he could win the next two events, but his ankle hurt so much. Nevertheless, he had insisted that the coach wrap his ankle, and he proceeded to compete in his last two events. He lost. He came in second place by a fraction of a second in the first of the events, but to him it had been a thunderous defeat. His spirit was broken. He came in dead last for his second event. He told Victoria that when he arrived home that evening, he had stood for a long time on the doorstep outside in the rain, paralyzed by shame and fear. He had thrown his second-place trophy into the bushes. Dan said he heard his parents yelling at each other as usual when he opened the door. His father walked over to him.

"Well?" his father had bellowed.

"I came in second." Dan had responded stoically.

"Never good enough for first, are you?" His father had laughed.

"John," his wife had urged, "please don't involve him in this!"

"He's already involved! When the hell is he going to become a man and start making some money for this family? He needs to forget those goddamned sports and get a job! I'm sick of working for everybody else! I've had it!"

Dan couldn't remember the rest of the fight. But it didn't matter. The damage had been done. Dan remembered his father slamming the door behind him as he walked out to his car in the rain. Dan had stood in the doorway and watched his father leave. From that point on, he had become the man of the house.

"Wow," Gabrielle sighed. "Heavy stuff for a kid."

"Yeah," Victoria said. "Kind of puts your own life into perspective. I mean, my childhood wasn't ideal with my parents' divorce and the two deaths, but we had always loved each other and encouraged each other. My parents had certainly never made me feel worthless."

They were both silent for a moment, reflecting on their own

childhoods.

"Okay," Gabrielle said, interrupting Victoria's thoughts. "So what else was there about him? Was he married? Or had he ever been married? Children?"

"Okay, okay! Back to my story of our first date, if you can call it that. And yes, he had been married and separated for almost two years when I met him."

"Not divorced?"

"Not divorced. I think that he had never quite wanted to get the final papers signed just in case."

"In case of what?" Gabrielle asked.

"In case he was faced with commitment again with some other woman. He would always have a back door, you know?"

"What does this mean, back door?"

Victoria remembered that her friend didn't always understand American expressions.

"A back door means he'd always have a way out if he got scared and didn't want to commit to someone else. He could always use the legal marriage as an excuse."

"Is that why you kept this relationship a secret? Because you were afraid he would use this back door to get away from you?"

"I suppose so. I mean, he really was legally separated. They lived in separate homes, and his wife had even moved on with another man. Anyway, let me get back to my story about the first date."

Gabrielle continued to listen intently as Victoria resumed telling her about her mystery man. She explained that Dan had married at the age of twenty-seven, and his wife had only been twenty-years-old. He met his wife when he was working for a small architectural firm as an intern after college. He had been working there and taking classes at night to become an architect. Apparently the firm where he was working held annual picnics, and that was where he had met Alisa, his ex-wife. She had walked right up to him while he was sitting on a bench eating a hotdog and had asked him to join her and the other employees of the firm in a softball game.

Dan had told Victoria that he had been stunned by Alisa's beauty and that he found himself following her speechlessly onto the softball field that day. After a short but appropriate courtship, they had married and then had a son, Adam. Dan shared that he had continued to work hard and eventually fought his way up to the top of the company. He bought a house and then sold it for a larger one. The perfect family. Almost. Dan had also felt that something was missing. He had worked so hard to put all the pieces of his life together, but when all had been accomplished, and there were no pieces of the puzzle remaining, he had realized that there was still a big gaping hole in the middle of the puzzle. He said he slowly went back to examine what he had overlooked. Had the missing pieces been stolen while he had been away from home working so hard all those years? He recounted that he started to spend more time with Adam. He attended his son's baseball and swim meets. He signed his son up for some neighborhood races and took him for ice-cream when the races were done. He celebrated his son's successes, no matter how small, and he didn't belittle him. He made a big deal about Adam's drawings and he hung them in his office. He had thought he could recuperate the time he had missed by spending more time with Alisa as well, but it had been too late. She had her own life, and he was not in it. Those were the pieces of the puzzle he did not have, and he didn't know if someone else had taken them, or if they were just hidden and would surface later on in the relationship. They never did. Alisa left the home shortly thereafter.

Victoria explained to her friend that Dan had decided much like herself that he had needed to fill a void, so he decided to start running again just as he had done in high school and college. He began with some local 5K races, and then he eventually found himself driving to Pennsylvania and New York to run more competitively. He was elected as president of the running club for his county, and he helped organize and officiate at races. A coach from Georgetown University met him after a race one day and asked him to co-author a book on training for races. He did, and the book sold quite well. But it wasn't enough. He told Victoria that he had never known what was missing from his life until he met her.

Gabrielle excused herself to go to the bathroom, leaving Victoria alone with her thoughts about that perfect evening in Old Town Alexandria.

Victoria remembered how Dan had taken her hand and had led her upstairs to the piano bar after they had finished dinner. He ordered a Rémy Martin, and it was served in a cognac glass warmed by a glowing fire. Victoria had stayed with the Chardonnay. She could still see Dan's face clearly in her mind as he had joked a bit with the bartender about the glass on fire. As she watched him, she had wondered what was hiding and yet to be revealed behind those fiery blue eyes of his.

Victoria recalled that as they walked back towards the car near the pier that evening, they could see the boats coming in to dock. They were magnificent. She had wondered what it would be like to be wealthy and to be a passenger on one of those boats. And yet, what could be richer than those precious moments standing on the dock with that wonderful man?

Dan had put his arms around her as they faced out towards the darkened waters, and she had leaned back into his chest. They had stood there for an eternity. She could almost feel his chin resting on her head and his arms warmly enveloping her.

"Have you ever felt this way before?" he had asked. She hadn't responded right away. "Tell me!" he urged.

"I know that I don't want tonight to end," she had replied honestly. It would be so difficult returning to the details of her life after that night. She had known that her life would never be the same.

"I love you," she had heard him whisper. It was clear. There was no mistake. It had been his voice.

"You love me too, don't you?" he had asked as he turned her to face him. "It's okay to tell me! You do, don't you?"

Victoria just didn't know what to say. This had been so unexpected, so fast, and yet it was what she had wanted, right? But so fast?

"Yes," she remembered saying.

# CHAPTER ELEVEN

"So where is he now?" Gabrielle gently interrupted her friend's thoughts as she returned to where they were sitting on the deck outside. "I brought the bottle out this time, by the way!" she said, pouring them both another glass of wine.

Gabrielle figured by Victoria's story that she must have met Dan about five years ago. She wondered why her friend had waited so long to tell her about him. And why the hell hadn't she guessed that someone was in Victoria's life? Or was he still in her life?

Victoria felt like she had been lost in her story for hours, but it had only been about half an hour since they had left the dinner table.

"It's a long story, Gabi. Maybe I should wait until tomorrow to continue."

"No! It is only six o'clock in the morning in France right now. It's early!"

"My point exactly!" exclaimed Victoria. "It's six o'clock the next day, and you haven't had any sleep!"

Gabrielle looked at her friend imploringly.

"Okay! Okay! I'll continue the story," she conceded. She loved Gabrielle. Her friend was concerned and Victoria was actually feeling relieved about finally sharing her story with someone.

"Why do people have affairs, anyway, Gabi?" Victoria asked her friend before continuing her story.

"You mean while they are married?"

"I guess it doesn't matter; either married or single. Why do married people have affairs, and why do singles have these relationships that they know full well won't turn into marriages?"

"Well," her friend replied, "maybe some people are just

always searching for that elusive love that you see in the movies and they don't recognize it when they have it. We get so confused when we leave the honeymoon behind and we enter the world of parenting, work, paying bills and responsibilities. It could just be a way of coping with all the stress. Maybe people feel lonely in their world of work and responsibilities. Perhaps some people feel the weight on their shoulders, and the spouse at home isn't too supportive. And sometimes I think we just get caught up in the moment and we don't think clearly about consequences or about hurting other people. I don't believe there is a set reason, though."

"What about single people? Why do they get involved when they know it won't lead anywhere?"

"They probably just get lonely. Maybe they feel hopeless after several years of being single, and they take the first promise of a relationship as their future hope. They don't listen to their own logic telling them that the relationship is not destined for a long term commitment. And then maybe some people just don't care. Perhaps they don't have time for long term things. Sometimes I think that people in our society are taught to aspire for more, for greater heights in their jobs, for more money, bigger houses, shinier cars, a more secure future, and perhaps for better mates. So they just keep looking for better mates, and they don't have time for commitment along the way."

"Shit. Why can't people just settle for a bigger car?" They both laughed.

"Life isn't very simple, is it Vicky?" her friend became serious again. "I really don't have any answers, and I'm not so sure there are any. Each case is different. Sometimes I feel like we should follow our hearts, but that is the impulsive me talking. Other times I know there are obligations we must fulfill and pro-mises we must keep. I know there has to be a balance somewhere."

"So you don't think people have affairs for love?"

"Sometimes. Did you truly love this man, Vicky?"

Victoria held her chin in both hands and leaned forward in her chair with her elbows on her knees. "I just don't know anymore. But the experience definitely had an effect on me. It scared me, to tell you the truth. Now I don't even want to date anymore. Can you tell me what true love is, Gabi?"

"No."

"But you and Pierre-Louis ..."

"Pierre is a wonderful companion, Vicky. I love him as the father of our two adorable children and he is a good provider and is supportive of my work," she smiled and then added "And he is great in bed!" They both laughed.

"What else is there?" Victoria asked.

"I don't know the answer. I only know that the question itself perplexes me every now and then. It complicates things a little when we women get in those little moods of ours and ask those questions, but it is actually when I am able to produce my best paintings. So I guess it all works out in the end!"

"Well, I don't like it. It hurts to love."

"Okay, so what happened after Old Town Alexandria?"

"Nothing. Well, not right away. He didn't call after that night."

Victoria proceeded to tell Gabrielle about the four or five months that followed that night. Dan never called. She didn't even know how to reach him to ask why, and she didn't want Carl to know that she had gone out with Dan. She was devastated as the days had gone by. But how silly! After only one date she was devastated?! Finally she had decided to put it aside in a corner of her mind as she had done so many times before with past sad events in her life, and she decided to throw herself into her training for the Olympic trials. With this new resolve she set in motion a training schedule that unleashed significant gains in running longer distances faster than ever before. She couldn't have known what Dan was going through while she was training for that race.

It had been many months after her evening with Dan, and Victoria had been preparing for the U.S. Women's Olympic

Marathon trials. She was on her way with Carl to South Carolina, and it was three days before the event. She felt very confident, because she knew she had trained well. Dan had been right, Carl was an excellent trainer. She had wanted to go to the games in August, and she knew she had a good chance of staying with the top three runners of this race in order to get there.

"Victoria," Carl had said as they neared their hotel in South Carolina. "I almost forgot! Dan asked me to give you this note when we got to South Carolina."

She had stared at him as if not comprehending what he had just said. Carl put the note in her hand. Victoria remembered gazing down at the letter not knowing whether to open it or save it for after the race. What could Dan have possibly said in the letter to take back all the anguish she had been put through when he hadn't even had the fortitude to call her and tell her that he didn't want to see her again?! She remembered feeling resentful. How dare he interfere with her race?

When they had checked in at the hotel, Victoria had vengefully thrown the letter into a drawer and had gone to dinner with Carl. But when she was getting ready for bed that night, she opened the drawer to get her pajamas, and she saw the envelope again. She just had to know. She had to know why he had never called. Not that it mattered now. But if she had had the courage to open her heart to Dan, then she certainly had the courage to open a piece of paper.

My Dear Victoria,

I cannot tell you how sorry I am for not being in touch with you all of these months. I will explain it someday, but I will not blame you for hating me and throwing me away.

This is your race, Victoria. Be patient and remember

all that you have practiced. Believe in yourself, and I know you will make it. I will be at the finish line.

I love you with all my heart,

Dan

Victoria came in third place at the trials the next day and was headed to the Olympics. She remembered reading somewhere that physical pain takes the mind off what really hurts inside. The physical pain she had felt had definitely kept her focused on the race. She remembered that when she finished the race, she was slightly dehydrated, but she had felt strong and grateful to see everyone waiting for her at the finish line. Dan was there as well, and she had smiled at him across the crowd as she had hugged her coach and her children and friends at the line. Then she lost sight of him in the crowd, but it hadn't mattered, because she knew he would call.

"I remember that day at the trials! I was there too!" said Gabrielle as they continued their talk on the deck.

"I know. It was right before you went back to France to open your art gallery."

"But I don't remember meeting Dan or even seeing him."

"You didn't. He disappeared from the crowd at the race so that I could be with family and friends and celebrate. But he did call. I saw him again, and this is where so much changed for me, Gabi."

# CHAPTER TWELVE

The weeks that had followed the Olympic trials were consumed by grueling training sessions and intense preparation for Victoria. Everyone was calling her and asking about flight reservations to go and watch her compete in the Olympics. Could she get them stadium tickets? What about some good rates at a hotel? Could she send them a map of the marathon route so they would know where to stand and cheer? Could she get some of those Olympic souvenir pins? Questions, questions, questions!

"How much money is this race worth?" her ex-husband had asked one day when he brought her a check to pay for his half of Christopher's college tuition. They were still in that phase of separation before the divorce was finalized. Although he was still bitter about the separation, they were getting along much better as partners in raising the children. It had been almost a year.

"None," she had responded. "A champion's worth is measured by her courage, and the purse is unimportant."

"Aren't money and worth the same thing?" he had reciprocated.

Tom had not been the only one that didn't understand why Victoria was pursuing this elusive championship or how it could have anything to do with courage and character. Most of her friends thought that it was stupid. The woman's marathon was still not a well-established event at the Olympics, and women were still being criticized. Some officials still harbored the idea that women were not physically built for this type of endurance, and that they would hurt themselves if they pushed too hard. All of the misconceptions had been debated years before, but the underlying belief was still there. Some people felt that this event for women only took away from the glory of the men's race, and that it made a mockery of the men's event by insinuating that women were as capable as they were.

Before Tom and Victoria had been talking about divorce, he had figured that Victoria had given up the notion to run in races when she had been raising their children. She had hardly ever competed in any races once the children came along, maybe just one or two small 5K races a year, and an occasional jog with some neighborhood friends. He had thought that she was just keeping up with her exercise. But when Victoria began running again when the children entered middle school and high school, Tom knew that they had grown apart. It had been at that time that he realized she was replacing him with running, and he hadn't known what to do. He eventually left her alone in hopes that she would just stay with the relationship. Maybe if they didn't talk about it, it would be fine. But it wasn't fine.

Victoria had minimized her distractions after the trials so that she could concentrate on the training. Mental preparedness was just as important as the physical endurance. She spent time only with her children and her coach. And Dan.

Dan had sent forty-eight daisies wrapped with a yellow satin ribbon to her home the day she arrived back in Maryland after the Olympic trials. The card had read *"forty-eight hours to recover, and then I'll meet you on the track on Tuesday at 8:00am."* There had been no signature on the card, but she knew it was him, and she knew she would be there.

# CHAPTER THIRTEEN

The evening at Old Town Alexandria had been one of the most wonderful evenings of his life, Dan had thought to himself. Meeting Victoria had helped him realize why he and his wife had separated several years prior; he had been in a loveless marriage where they both had lost sight of why they had married in the first place. Since the separation, he had just been existing, with no real interest to date anyone he had met so far. No one was worth the time, that is, until Victoria entered his life. He had thrown himself into his work and building the new house he had designed for himself. The house was now nearing completion. Victoria could give him what he had yearned for and what had been missing from his fifteen-year marriage to Alisa: friendship, companionship, sympathy.

But Dan was still wary about another serious relationship so soon after his separation. Alisa had viewed the separation differently than he, and she had been the first to discuss the issues that she felt had drawn them apart. He hadn't agreed with her at all. She told him that he had been too hard on her, that he had always expected more, and that she felt she had always been on the edge of not being perfect enough for him. He had responded that he had simply wanted her to maximize her potential because he wanted other people to see what he had seen in her. Alisa tried to explain that it was more than that. She had always tried to keep up that image that seemed so important to him. She had worn just the types of clothes he had wanted her to wear, for example. And she had agreed to always wear heels around him because he had this thing about wanting her to be tall. She had wanted to wear flats, because it really didn't matter how tall she was. He thought that she had liked wearing what he had picked out for her. He couldn't understand why she said she felt like he was only interested in a trophy wife. She was about seven years younger than he, and he had been tremendously proud of her when other men turned their heads to stare as they went by. The sex was great, and he knew other men were envious. But the friendship and warmth had not been cultivated in their marriage. They had had a son too soon after they got married. As the years passed, they had begun to argue more and more over these insignificant details. He had complained about the house being untidy, and she had wanted to spend time with her son and friends instead of cleaning the house. He had wanted dinner on the table when he came home, and she and their son had already eaten because Dan came home too late for them to wait. Neither had seemed to understand the disagreements or the patterns they were creating. They just kept pushing each other away. Eventually Alisa told him that she needed some time apart. She had said she needed time to figure out who she was without him telling her who she was. He still didn't understand what she had been saying. They both moved into separates homes for the next two years, and he had waited.

The morning after meeting Victoria for dinner in Old Town, Dan had decided to go see his lawyer to talk about finalizing a divorce from Alisa. It was time. Maybe this relationship would be different. They could re-invent themselves and leave old baggage and bad habits behind. He would be more attentive, more caring. He wouldn't be so controlling, as Alisa had claimed. Maybe he had been a little bit that way because Alisa had been so much younger, or maybe because he had inherited it from his father. But now that he was aware, he'd make sure to not make the same mistakes. He appreciated Victoria for exactly who she was

Victoria hadn't known about the visit to the lawyers. She only knew that he had remained separated for several years for whatever reasons that she had no right to ask. In the months that followed the visit to the lawyers, Dan and Alisa began the back and forth negotiations and conditions for the divorce. He then learned from his lawyer that Alisa was planning to move to Boston and that she had requested custody of Adam. Dan was shocked. He hadn't seen that coming. Alisa had met someone and was moving to Boston to be near this new man in her life. Dan couldn't let that happen! The lawyer had sat with him for a long time and planned their strategy to prevent Alisa from taking Adam to Boston. The list of instructtions to Dan included not dating anyone for the time being so that Alisa couldn't drag someone else into her battle. He was not to be seen drinking or partying in clubs, he was told to rent a small house or apartment while his was being built so that his son could have a room of his own, and he was to adjust his work schedule so that he would be gone in the morning only after Adam would be in school. He had to be home on a regular basis in the evenings. That didn't mean that those strategies would work, or that he would have to stick to them in the long run, but for the time being, the lawyer had wanted him to be cautious.

Dan had walked for a very long time in the city after talking to the lawyer that day. He did not want to lose his son. He was angry at Alisa, even though he understood how she could have fallen for someone else, because he had fallen for Victoria. But he couldn't start a relationship right now, could he? *What was he thinking*? How could he work for the company all day, work in the evenings on the house he was building, move into another house while he was building it, take care of Adam, and start a dating relationship all at once? Was he nuts?! How could he ever explain to Victoria that he would need to put the new relationship on hold? It was like joining the CIA and then just meeting someone special as you learned that your next assignment would be to disappear for a year without a trace. Would the person wait for you? Was there that much trust fostered at such an early stage of a relationship to ask the other person to wait for what may never evolve into anything later? No, he couldn't ask Victoria to wait. She was training for the Olympic trials, and if he got her involved in all of this mess, it would be such a distraction. He had already ruined

Alisa's life by expecting her to be everything he had wanted, so he wasn't going to repeat the same mistake with Victoria. He was going to give her the space she needed to become the champion she had to be, and then he would see if she was still willing to give him a chance. He just didn't want to leave her without telling her something, anything. He went home and called her the next day. No answer. He called her three times before he decided that the call was not meant to be. If she had answered, he didn't even know what he would have said. He decided to stop calling.

# CHAPTER FOURTEEN

Gabrielle and Victoria continued their talk the next morning over coffee. Gabrielle had tossed and turned all night trying to shake the last remnants of jet-lag. As she lay there awake that night, Gabrielle had made a mental list of all the questions she would ask her friend about her story in the morning.

"So did he get to keep his son?" Gabrielle started while sipping her coffee.

"What? Oh, you mean did Dan get to keep Adam? Yes. Dan and Alisa battled it out for months. After that, for whatever reason, Alisa decided not to move to Boston."

"She realized the guy in Boston was a jerk?"

"No, she realized that Adam was more important. She figured that if the guy in Boston really loved her that he'd wait for a year until Adam graduated from high school and then she would join him when Adam went to college. Dan and Alisa got joint custody and they lived not too far from each other, actually. It all worked out in the end."

"So what about you and Dan?"

"Well, we got together and talked the whole thing out after the Olympic trials. I was so busy training, though, that we hardly had any time together at that point. We talked on the phone as much as possible and wrote each other long letters late into the night. He wrote so beautifully! I never stopped to think about what I was doing, you know? I just let it happen."

"Let what happened?" Gabrielle asked.

"I allowed myself to fall in love."

"And then what?" her friend pressed on.

"And then came the car accident. Remember?" Victoria tilted her head frowning.

"I'll never forget," her friend responded softly.

"Listen," said Victoria quickly, "I've got to go to the store. Can we continue this later?"

"Promise?"

"Yes, I promise!"

"So is there sex in part two of this story?" her friend asked to lighten the mood while laughing.

"You are incorrigible, Gabi!"

Victoria and Gabrielle never found the time in the remainder of the day to continue their conversation. But by the time Victoria finally lay in bed that night after a long day at work, she couldn't stop thinking about where she had left off with her story that morning with Gabi. She thought about the events leading to the Olympic Games, the games in which she never competed.

# CHAPTER FIFTEEN

"What are you doing?!" Carl had asked Victoria one day as they were halfway through a speed workout to get ready for the Olympics.

"What do you mean?" Victoria had asked, breathing deeply.

"You're dragging your left leg again!" her coach had responded.

"My knee. I know, I know. It's acting up again, Carl." She hadn't wanted to tell him because she knew he'd make her take off some time, and she couldn't afford to take off time at that point.

"You're taking two days off. Your vacation starts now." He was serious.

Victoria could remember as clear as if it had been yesterday what had happened next. She was one month away from the Olympics, but she knew that her coach had been right about the two-day rest. So she had decided to ask her sister Rina if they could use her cabin at Deep Creek Lake, about three hours away from the city, to get her mind off of her training.

"Let's go visit aunt Rina's cottage in Deep Creek!" Victoria had said to her daughter Jennifer. "I have two days off from training. We'll have a slumber party and get aunt Rina to take off from her job in Baltimore to join us. We can get a bunch of junk food and rent movies and swim in the lake!"

Victoria remembered that she had actually been glad that she had taken some time off, and she was looking forward to this little trip with her daughter and her sister. Jennifer was ecstatic. Rina had reluctantly agreed to take the time off to go with them, but then the idea grew on her as well. Rina had a beautiful quaint little cottage in the country near the lake in southern Maryland where she escaped on occasion from the cacophony of the city when it got really bad. The cottage had belonged to Rob's grandparents. Victoria and Jennifer had affectionately called it *Terra* and always loved pretending they were spoiled characters from *Gone with the Wind* when they went there.

The morning after their first night at the cottage filled with popcorn and M&Ms and pizza, Victoria and Jennifer had decided to go out for a short jog, just two miles. Not enough to make her coach angry or to hurt her knee, but enough to get that junk food out of her system. It would be a nice way to spend time with her daughter and catch up on all her activities at school.

It had been a beautiful crisp morning. The sky was a light blue dotted by occasional clouds, and the mist had just begun to dissipate. The smell of honeysuckle pierced the morning air as Victoria and Jennifer set out for their easy run along country roads, dodging squirrels and moles and awakening the bees for their busy day of work. Jennifer had chatted incessantly about her friends, books, clothes, and boys. Boys, Victoria remembered thinking. *When had that happened?* She missed the short runs she used to do with her daughter. The training sessions for the Olympics had been getting too long and grueling, so they had not been able to run together for awhile.

The shoulder on the country roads had been somewhat narrow, so when a car would approach, they would run in a single file. The local folks were kind people, and when they saw runners or cyclists in the roads, they would veer away from them towards the middle so as not to pose a danger to them. This morning, however, a single car did not veer away.

Victoria had seen an oncoming car continue on a path straight towards them, and the car didn't seem to be moving away from the shoulder. It was odd that a car would wait until the last minute to move towards the middle of the lane. There wasn't any oncoming traffic. There weren't any other cars on the road, as a matter of fact. She knew that they were both within the white line of the shoulder area, and she had told Jennifer to form a single file. The car wasn't moving away. Victoria last remembered screaming and pushing Jennifer into the bushes on the side as she made eye contact with the driver. Then there was only blackness.

Victoria remembered the long painful recovery after the accident that deprived her of her dream to participate in the Olympics.

Rebecca had rushed to the hospital with Rina's husband as soon as they had heard the news of the accident. Her eyes had been puffy and dark, and her sixty three years were showing more than ever. *You're not supposed to outlive your children*, she had thought to herself. Yet here she was in the hospital again with one more daughter near her death. Esperanza's death had been so difficult, and she didn't know if she could endure the heartbreak if Victoria did not recover from this accident. Rebecca had gotten up and walked out to the waiting room to check on Christopher and Jennifer. They had been sleeping in the plastic hospital chairs. Rebecca got some blankets from the nurse to put over them. Jennifer had been bruised from falling into the bushes, but she had insisted on staying near her mother's room. They had all been waiting for two days. Two days, and Victoria had not yet come out of a coma. It had been hard to tell what internal damage might have occurred since she hadn't regained consciousness after the car had hit her.

"She's stable," the doctors had said. "We can't tell yet what will happen. We know that she will recover from the hip surgery she needs and she should be able to walk fine. Her arm will also mend. The bruises are deep and will be painful for awhile. Right now we just need to wait for her to regain consciousness. It's hard to tell when that will happen, but we don't see any reason why there should be any brain damage. We did have to go in on one side and drain …" Rebecca had suddenly felt dizzy. Tom had been there and he walked her over to a chair. Gabrielle had also been there and brought her some coffee.

Carl had listened intently to the doctor's report, and then walked down the hall and down two flights of stairs in the hospital where he met Dan who had been waiting for the news.

"Dan, it really is okay for you to go up there. You were her coach too, in a sense. Introduce yourself to her family as a coach."

"No," Dan had replied.

The newspaper in the local town had written a small blurb about the accident on page four. It reported the mishap as a hit and run incident. The reporter was calling it purposeful, and he wrote a paragraph on a new thing called *road rage*. Psychologists were calling this road rage a mental disorder, according to the reporter. Something would trigger frustration, and then the person would act out in violent behavior. There were reports of other men taking to cars to escape their rage, and these episodes sometimes resulted in violent crashes. Apparently cases had increased by fifty percent over the past four years. Victoria had just been a victim of some displaced anger.

That afternoon, a young girl not more than fifteen years old, had stepped out of the elevator and walked into the waiting room where Victoria's family had been waiting for news from the doctors.

"Which one is the daughter?" she had whispered to the nurse at the desk.

"That one in the corner," the nurse had motioned. "Are you with the family?"

"Kind of," she answered.

The girl had walked over to Jennifer.

"Hi," she had said barely audible. She had begun to cry, but had kept her composure. "My father was the hit-and-run driver that struck your mom on the road on Monday."

Jennifer had gasped in disbelief and had been unable to say anything.

"I was in the car," the girl continued. I went to the police this morning. I'm so sorry!" she heaved forward with a burst of tears while covering her face.

Jennifer grabbed the girl by the shoulders and looked angrily into her eyes wanting to shake her and hate her for all the pain the girl's father had inflicted on her own family. But she saw through the windows of her eyes a pain that equaled her own. They were both victims. They were both losing a parent. She pulled the girl towards her and hugged her as they both wept.

"*JENNIFER!*" The shrill scream had come from Victoria's hospital room. She was waking up and had suddenly remembered what had happened. "Where is my Jennifer?!" she cried out to anyone who might have been in the hallway to hear.

"She's back!" Carl had whispered to himself when he heard Victoria screaming for her daughter. He ran down the hall to make his report to Dan who had not left the hospital in two days.

Recovery had been slow following her hip surgery, but Victoria was a stubborn and resolute person, and her strong will had gotten her through the ordeal well enough to finally be able to go home.

One week after returning from the hospital, Victoria had watched the Women's Olympic Marathon on television alone in her bedroom. Among the many stories being aired during the marathon about the contestants, a reporter shared Victoria's story. He talked about how Victoria had been a major contender, and how she had been tragically struck and had been forced to remove her number from the race.

"This could have been Victoria's run," he had reported.

Victoria had gasped and cried uncontrollably. She was angry and helpless and frustrated. She had relived the accident over and over in her mind and thought about what she could have done to avoid the car. She had been doing this for weeks, but she had always ended by praying and thanking God for having saved her daughter and for her own recovery. She could walk now with a cane, and she would continue to mend and would eventually be able to walk with a fairly normal gait. But she would never be able to run competitively again. The doctor had assured her that with time, she would be able to jog. But speed could never be the objective.

Victoria had felt like her life was falling apart. She felt like she had been losing control of everything, not just her ability to run. The trauma had exacerbated all the other issues that had been swirling around in her mind; things that she had put on a back burner while she had been training for the marathon. She began to question what had happened between her and Tom, what was happening with her and Dan, and whether she was spending enough time being a good mom to her children. She didn't want to repeat the same mistakes with Dan that she had made with Tom.

Dan had been divorced for such a short time, and Victoria felt guilty about asking for time with him when he was preoccupied with work, the construction on his house, and taking care of his son. Victoria and Dan still had not said anything to anyone about their relationship. Carl was the only one that knew. It had been such a recent thing, and they hadn't even given it a fair shot. Victoria had been training all that time while Dan had been working with his lawyer, and then the accident occurred, and he had felt uncomfortable coming to her house to see her. Then Alisa had decided not to go to Boston. Had that meant that maybe the two of them would reconcile? What a confusing relationship! Why couldn't they get their act together?!

Dan had been just as confused as Victoria. He had felt helpless as he was unable to see Victoria and take care of her while she was recovering. He had tried to go to the hospital when the family was not there. One time, however, her children had come in while he was visiting. Victoria introduced him to them as one of her coaches. It had looked innocent enough, as Dan had taken Adam there with him. Christopher had been impressed with the pilot's wings that Dan wore on his leather jacket, and Dan had briefly explained that he had taken classes and got his license to fly a small craft that he owned with a partner. Dan had wanted to ask Christopher to come and fly with him and Adam, especially since they were so close in age, but he restrained himself from asking. He had figured that it was too soon for either family to be told that the parents were carrying on. Were they actually *carrying on*, he wondered to himself. They hadn't spent too much time together. After reconnecting right after the Olympic trials, they had written each other many long letters and tried to sneak in conversations on the phone, but there had not been too much time to see each other. They had never actually gone out on a date after the one in Old Town. They'd seen each other sporadically on the track, and Carl had guessed why Dan had wanted to come and help him train Victoria.

Friends had started asking Dan why he wouldn't accept offers to be introduced to their female friends. People knew that he had initiated the official divorce. But he kept saying that he wasn't ready to date yet. He was committed emotionally to Victoria, so how could he go out with anyone else? He had shared all his thoughts with her as he went through the final stages of divorce, and he had told her all his insecurities and fears. He had given himself to her completely, and he wasn't even sure she understood how difficult that had been for him. He wanted her, and he did not want to keep living without her. The nights were lonely, and the weekends that Adam went to stay with his mother had become frustrating hours of waiting and hoping that Victoria would have a few private moments in which to call him and talk. He shouldn't be living like this, not after close to three years of separation from Alisa. But the guilt of pursuing any female friendship, no matter how innocuous, was unthinkable. He felt disloyal and unfaithful with the mere consideration of going on a meaningless date with someone for platonic sociability.

Victoria had cherished every minute she could be with Dan. He had become her hope and her advisor. He had taught her to be strong and to not walk away from adversity. He had taught her to be a champion by pushing herself beyond her limits while she was training. There *were* no limits.

Victoria had wanted him, even though she understood his conflict. But what *was* the conflict, she had wondered. Dan was well into his first year of divorce from Alisa. His son Adam had been settling into his new life of having divorced parents, and Dan had been getting ready to move into his newly finished house. So it wasn't too soon for people to think that he had just met someone, she thought. Victoria and Tom had also been well on their way to finalizing their divorce proceedings. But she agreed with Dan to keep the relationship a secret a bit longer, for whatever reason. After all, when you get divorced for reasons that no one understands, people begin to conjecture and accuse. Victoria and Tom both knew that they had grown apart long ago, just as Dan and Alisa had, but she didn't want to leave any room for gossip. She wouldn't want her children to ever wonder about her motives or actions.

Victoria had felt guilty that she had been keeping Dan from living his life while she was recovering from her surgery and getting her own life in order with her children and her house. What if he woke up one morning and realized that he had been giving away precious moments of his life with no hope for the future? Would he resent her for this loss?

One year later, Victoria had fully recovered from her injuries and had moved into a comfortable pattern in her life once more. She was officially divorced, and the lawsuit against the violent driver had been settled. She was teaching again at the university,

Christopher had been doing well in his first year of college, and Jennifer was enjoying her early years of high school.

Victoria had been meeting Dan whenever they had had a free evening when Jennifer was with her father and Chris and Adam were at college. She had finally felt that it was time to bring their relationship out in the open, but Dan discouraged her from doing so. She couldn't understand why he had continued to keep it a secret. He had been talking all year about the frustration of not being able to go out in public for dinner or to a movie, but lately he had been cold on the idea of talking to the children and their families about their relationship. There had been enough time now for the relationship to grow, and Victoria was certain that Dan would be in her life forever. She had spend the last year learning all about him and helping him get established in his new home while Adam was away at college. She loved his new house. He was truly a talented architect. She was pretty good at decorating, so she spent her free time decorating his home and buying items to create a warm and inviting feeling. Dan loved it. Victoria would come over right after work and would iron his shirts, clean the bathrooms, buy little plants for his windows, put up curtains, or just move things around until they felt right in the rooms. She'd often surprise him by baking cookies and leaving them on a tray for when he came home in the evening tired from work. He'd call her and thank her every time. Victoria knew that these were the small details that meant so much to Dan, and that his house would not truly be a home without them.

Finally Victoria had decided that it was time to tell the world that she was in love, even if Dan had not quite been ready for the revelation. No more secrets, she had decided. She wanted her life to be normal again. Victoria had walked to Dan's office after work to surprise him. She had never gone there unannounced before, because they had both wanted to avoid having his co-workers question him about her before they were both ready to explain who she was. She couldn't tell people he was her coach anymore, because she wasn't running anymore. This day she felt happier than she had ever been and she had wanted to surprise him. What the heck? It was as good a time as ever to begin telling people that they were actually dating.

She walked into his office and saw the brunette in his arms. She walked out and never saw him again.

# CHAPTER SIXTEEN

"Vicky, *reveille toi*! Its wake-up time!" yelled Gabrielle cheerfully up the stairs the next morning. It was Friday morning, and she didn't want to sleep away the hours. They had definitely stayed up too late the previous night visiting with Rina and her husband, but nonetheless Gabrielle felt refreshed and ready to go.

Jennifer and Gabrielle were already dressed and were at the kitchen table. Jennifer was eating pancakes that Gabrielle had made for her, and they were talking about her senior Prom that evening and about Christopher's graduation from college next weekend. Realizing it was getting late, Jennifer started packing her book bag for school and putting her dishes in the sink.

"How am I going to do this, Aunt Gabrielle?" Jennifer asked. "I have a playoff game for the softball championship that doesn't end until 5:30 or 6:00 tonight, and I'm supposed to be at the restaurant at 7:00 to meet my date and the rest of my group! How am I going to get my hair done? I can't believe we won on Wednesday and now we have to play this game on Prom night!!! The coach said that if the seniors don't show for the game, we can't play in the finals. And I'm the pitcher!" Jennifer was in a panic, and the more she talked, the more she got herself riled up.

"Okay, okay, one thing at a time. Now, when can you get out of school today?"

"We have to stay until noon to comply with the attendance regulation so that we can play in the game this afternoon." Jennifer was confident that Gabrielle would figure out what to do next, because she was good at plotting and planning.

"Okay, so I'll pick you up right at twelve. We'll go to Victor's for your hair, and I think your aunt Rina wanted to meet us for lunch."

"Who is Victor?" Jennifer asked.

"Ahhh, Victor. Who is he *not*? He can do wonders with yucky hair and he can fix nails like you won't believe!"

"What if I break a nail at the game?!" Jennifer interrupted.

"Don't even worry about it! I know how to fix them!"

"Well how do I do my hair if I have to wear a helmet at the game?"

"You know what? All those hairdos with all those curls on top of the head and hair full of spray are really overrated. Don't worry. Victor can trim your hair in a soft straight style that will caress your shoulders and will cascade down the middle of your back! Yes, and we'll ask for a few gentle highlights, too."

"Highlights?! Mom will kill me!" Jennifer lowered her voice and laughed.

"Unobtrusive ones! No one will be the wiser!"

"I love you, Aunt Gabrielle!" She hugged her mother's friend, grabbed her bag, and ran out the door to her car so she wouldn't be late to school.

"Did I miss her?" Victoria asked her friend as she walked into the kitchen.

"*Oui*. Gone. Do you teach any classes today at the university?"

"No. But I have to go in for a couple of hours to work on a research project. Do you want to come with me? There are some nice little shops around the university that you might like. You could wander around a bit and then we could meet for lunch."

"I have a lunch date with your daughter," laughed Gabrielle. "But if we go soon, we can make it for a late breakfast and then I can get back on time to meet Jennifer. She took her car to school, so I guess I won't pick her up, and I'll just meet her here."

"Oh, no. What are you going to do with Jen?" Victoria laughed. Remember that she has a game this afternoon, and that we have to get her ready for the Prom right after the game!"

"Don't worry! I'm just going to go with her to get her hair

and nails done. Nothing weird, I promise!"

"Okay, just get her back by 3:00 for the game. Oh, and Tom is coming over to take some pictures before she rushes over to the restaurant." God, Victoria pleaded under her breath, please don't let Jennifer show up to the game with green hair! Gabrielle and Rina spoiled this girl rotten, and Victoria loved it, she thought to herself shaking her head back and forth and smiling.

At 10:30am Gabrielle met Victoria outside the café near the university for their brunch. May had turned out to be a beautiful month---not too hot and not too cold. There were flowers blooming everywhere around the restaurant in shades of orange, purple and yellow.

After a sip of her Mimosa, Gabrielle decided that it was time to ask her friend for the rest of her story about this mysterious man that stole her heart, cheated on her with some other woman, and then left Victoria no choice but to leave him. It sounded like they weren't even officially an item to begin with. So why is she still thinking about him? It had to have been a couple of years ago, or at least a full year ago!

"So Dan came back for the Olympics. He was in your life during the year you were recuperating, you fell in love, and then you found him with some brunette."

"I guess it goes like that. It sounds so simple when you put it all together in one sentence. But it sure did complicate my life. I placed all my trust in him, Gabi."

"You'll be able to trust men again, Vicky, believe me. You just haven't found the right one yet."

"I'm really not cut out for long term relationships. Marriage and I just don't go together. Tom used to tell me I'm too independent. I think he liked that in me, but I also think that created some distance. I guess I just like to do everything myself,

94

you know? I was used to that growing up. I had to grow up fast, and I had to find my way."

"Vicky, it will come. Independence is not a reason to not get married again. By the way, off the topic, that's a pretty bracelet you're twirling on your wrist."

"Well, that's something I wanted to show you. Dan gave this to me. He gave it to me so that I'd remember that whenever I wore it, I'd know that someone cares about me, and I'd gather strength from it."

"So why did you let him go? Are you sure the brunette was a love interest and not a cousin or something?"

"I'm sure. It was probably for the best anyway …"

"Why do you say that?" asked Gabrielle.

"Well, on the one hand, the relationship was great. It was strong and reckless like this wild ivy that continued to grow in spite of everything that came into its path. And he loved listening to me, Gabi, to the details of my day. That was so important."

"That's true."

"He worried about me too, like when I'd be out late or go on a trip with the kids. Once I went caving with Christopher and some friends, and I thought that Dan was going to hyperventilate when I told him, because he was so worried about everything that could go wrong! I loved the attention and caring, though. But on the other hand, I felt smothered."

"Smothered?"

"I felt like I was becoming someone that wasn't me. We fought a lot, too. I wasn't really used to that. I'm just not the fighting type, you know? In retrospect, many of our battles were about our relationship. He wouldn't commit to talking about the future, even though he kept saying he couldn't ever let me go."

"I just don't get it."

"I know. And he had wanted me to help decorate his home; he said that he wanted me to eventually make it mine. But then one day he said that he just couldn't picture me in the kitchen of his house! It was so confusing to me."

"You don't need to be in his fucking kitchen anyway, *chère*. He can cook for himself!" They laughed.

After a moment, Victoria continued. "He would tell me he loved me, but he almost loved me too much. He was jealous, not just of other men, but of friendships I had with women. He wondered why women went out so much and spent so much time together. He wanted to know what we talked about. Everything, you know?"

"Oh, if he could only hear us talking now!" Gabrielle was trying to keep it light. "He would brood while I was gone, and then he'd try to push me away. Figuratively, that is. But then I'd walk away and he'd pull me back. I'd have to sweet talk him out of his moods. The make-up sessions were good," she laughed, "but I really got so tired of his brooding and his doubts. I had always been such a happy person by disposition, but his brooding was changing me. I couldn't understand why he had so many doubts about us, and then I started doubting myself. I thought that maybe I wasn't good enough for a man like him, and that maybe he was thinking that about me too."

"So what was his problem with just getting together and telling people?" Gabrielle finally asked. "Was there someone else in his life? Did you ever suspect?"

"I don't know. I guess after it was all over, I did suspect there had been someone else all along."

"How was that?" asked Gabrielle.

"Well, when I'd go to his house to help decorate or iron his shirts, he would turn off the ringer on the phone, or he'd turn off the message machine. He had said that he didn't want me to be disturbed by all his business calls. Towards the end he was nervous about me even being there. One time someone called, and he said it was Alisa, and that she wanted to bring something over for Adam. So he asked me to go sit in my car around the corner until she was gone. He called me on my cell phone about twenty minutes later and said the coast was clear. Is that a way for a divorced man to act?"

"There definitely had to be someone else," her friend responded.

"I'm just not sure. I asked him once."

"And what did he say?"

"Well, he denied it and acted all defensive and offended. It ended in one of those little fights we would have, so I dropped it. He was just so loving towards me, and he'd bring me little gifts after a fight, like this bracelet, so it was difficult to believe that he could be with anyone else. I just kept hanging on."

"Why? Did it ever occur to you that maybe he was calling all the time to check on where you were so that he could invite someone else over to his house while he knew you were with your kids or something? That he didn't want to get caught?"

"Really?" Victoria looked at her friend with this new information to digest. "No, I guess that never occurred to me."

"It's possible, Vicky. What I don't understand, and please don't take offense, is why you didn't ever leave if it was causing you so much frustration to be in this relationship?"

"I did leave, actually. Several times. We'd fight and I'd walk away and tell him not to call me ever again. But he'd pursue me. One time we went a week without talking and I thought it was over. I was almost relieved. But he just had this hold on me. He'd call and cry, or send flowers, or tell me sad stories. I guess I nurtured him because I needed nurturing too. Maybe I needed to feel like I wasn't a failure at relationships, so I would try to stick with it and try to fix it. I really became convinced that I was not good enough to be deserving of him, or any other man, Gabi. I know, it's crazy. And the worse part of it was that Dan would pick these stupid fights all the time and then make it look like it was my fault. I really started to believe that the fights *were* my fault, you know what I mean?"

"No, I don't. This was definitely not who you were. Did he

ever call to explain who the brunette was?"

"Yes. But I didn't answer the phone. Then he would come looking for me, but I made sure there were always people around, and I pretended not to see him. He never came to my house. He wrote letters, and I threw them away."

"Where is he now?"

"In Arizona." Gabrielle motioned for the waiter to bring the check.

"I'm missing something. How the heck did he get way over there?"

"His son Adam transferred over to the University of Arizona at the same time that Dan was offered some fantastic architectural contract connected with the Biosphere over in Oracle."

"Is he still there?"

"I think so, but I don't know. Adam and Chris actually met during that time that Dan and I were together. I had introduced him as my coach's son. They did a few things together, and I think they still keep in touch by e-mail or Facebook or something. Every now and then Chris will say something about Adam, but I don't feel comfortable asking about Dan. Anyway, his contract in Arizona was supposed to be for one year, but I think he may have stayed for a second year, because Adam didn't come back for the summer. Adam usually stops by to see Chris when he's here. Does that sound odd?"

"Probably a little weird for you, but no one else is the wiser."

The waiter returned to the table with the check and Victoria grabbed it before her friend could get it. "I'll pay. It's really late. You go get my daughter and have Victor do nice things with her hair!"

"*Mon Dieu!* You're right! I have to run!" Gabrielle exclaimed as she looked down at her watch and jumped out of her chair. "I told Rina I'd pick her up and take her with us too! Then you get to have Jennifer back after the game, mom."

"You two are such great aunties to Jen. I appreciate all you do, you know, and that you came all this way to visit and attend Christopher's graduation."

"You will always be my extended family, Vicky!" She bent down and kissed her friend on the head. "You don't have to finish the story if you don't want, but if you do, you know I'll be around later after my business dinner tonight in Baltimore, okay?"

Victoria sighed. "The story is finished, Gabi."

"I don't believe you. Anyway, I'll see you at three o'clock when I deliver our beautiful little princess to the softball game!"

Gabrielle ran off to her car and Victoria walked the five blocks back to her building nearby to finish a little work before going to the game. She had wanted to walk, she had told Gabrielle, so that she could enjoy the weather. Gabrielle had known that her friend just needed some time to think things through after their conversation, so she did not insist on giving her a ride back to the university.

# CHAPTER SEVENTEEN

The girls won their softball game, but even more amazing was that Jennifer didn't show up to the game with green hair! The highlights and haircut were very attractive, and Victoria was so proud of her daughter. The game was a quick one, and Jennifer rushed home to shower and dress for the prom.

Victoria was stunned at how beautiful Jennifer looked in her purple dress. As she was helping her daughter zip up the dress, Jennifer asked "How will I know if I am ever in love, mom?"

"Is this about the guy you're going to the prom with, Jen?"

"No mom!" she responded. "I just mean in general. How will I know?"

"You'll know when nothing else matters but him."

"Were you ever in love like the person in the story you wrote?" There it was. Jennifer hadn't forgotten the story. It had made more of an impact than Victoria had wished.

"There are lots of different kinds of love, sweetie." She avoided the question. "Is this Mark guy you're going with tonight a possibility?"

"Mom!" admonished Jennifer as she filled her satin purse with the essentials for the night. The doorbell rang.

"Mark!" exclaimed Jennifer in a panic. "Mom, go downstairs, please! We can't have dad with him there alone! Who knows what dad will say to him!" They both laughed. Tom had come over to their house to take pictures of Jennifer and a few other friends before they left for the restaurant. The rest of the group had already left to make sure they held the reservations for them.

Jennifer was gorgeous, Victoria mused. She was all grown up. How does that happen so quickly with just the blink of an eye? She closed her eyes for a moment as memories of Jennifer's childhood flashed past her: Jennifer learning to walk and pushing that little orange grocery cart around the court; her first day at pre-school carrying her little lunch box and eating her lunch as soon as she got there... She thought about all the little Halloween costumes, the birthday parties, and days in their big plastic pool out in the backyard.

Victoria opened her eyes and saw the most gorgeous young woman running towards her in the driveway to give her one last hug before leaving.

"Mom, I know you're going to cry!" They both laughed. "Love you, mom!"

Victoria stood in the driveway and waved goodbye until the car was out of sight.

The day following the prom was a lazy one. Victoria and Gabrielle hadn't spent much time together the night before because Victoria had fallen asleep on the sofa shortly after Jennifer and her friends had left for the prom and Gabrielle had gone to her business dinner in Baltimore. Now they both sat outside on the deck drinking coffee while Jennifer slept safely and soundly in her bedroom after coming home at four o'clock in the morning. The kids had gone to the after-prom activity sponsored by the parent association right after midnight, and that had lasted until three in the morning.

"So why did you wait so long to tell me your story, Vicky?" Gabrielle asked as she took a sip of her coffee.

"I don't know why I didn't tell you before. I should have. You certainly would have set me straight, right?" She laughed. "Well, like I said before, Dan had wanted us to continue keeping it to ourselves until the time was right. I guess the time just never was right. I was embarrassed, too. Embarrassed because it had been so soon after leaving Tom, and people would have surely gossiped about it. I didn't want to have to go through that or put the kids through that. I really hate gossip!"

"So if it is in the past, why this urgency to tell me now?"

"Because Jen found a story I had written about two years ago after I had left Dan. I'm not even sure why I wrote it, really. I guess I had wanted to re-write what had happened, or pretend that it had never happened, or just continue looking out the glass windows at children playing with geese."

"What? Children playing with geese?"

"Never mind," Victoria answered, "it's in the story." She smiled.

Victoria went into the kitchen and then came out with the mail and some more coffee.

"Anyway, Jennifer wants to know what love is, and to tell you the truth, I'm not the expert. So maybe that's why I wanted to tell you the story. I do feel relieved having told you, though. I feel like it wasn't so bad after putting it into words. It was just an experience, right? Just something in the past that helped me to grow."

Victoria looked down at the mail she had brought out earlier.

"Gosh, I was so busy yesterday that I didn't even get a chance to look at this stuff!"

She rifled through the mail, passing the newspaper to her friend. Then an envelope with a return address from Puerto Rico caught her eye.

"This is interesting," she said to Gabrielle. "Why would I be getting some letter all the way from Puerto Rico from the Cancer and Health Foundation?"

Gabrielle put down her coffee and newspaper and paid attention.

"Holy shit!" Victoria exclaimed after opening it. Gabrielle knew this had to be big, because Victoria never used curse words.

"Look at this!" Victoria said passing the letter to her friend.

"Vicky, you *have* to do this!" Gabrielle said after reading the letter and returning it to her friend. She stared at Victoria willing her to say yes.

A committee that organized marathons in Puerto Rico to benefit education and medical research was asking Victoria to come to the island for the summer and help them organize the first twenty-six mile marathon along the northern seaboard for early December. Apparently some of the members of the committee had remembered her as a teenager running that crazy distance in order to win her scholarship to UVA, and they found an article in the *San Juan Star* that verified her name and some more recent information about her. She had married and changed her name since running back in her teen years, but the *Star* had done a follow-up article on her when she had qualified for the Olympic trials. They wanted her to be the director, the coordinator, and they were requesting a meeting to discuss the salary.

Puerto Rico had joined the world of marathoning back in 1963 when Delta Phi Delta Fraternity organized the San Blas Half-Marathon to honor the founder of the small town of Coamo.

"The Coamo race has become a major event with international and elite runners and has raised a lot of money," Victoria explained to Gabrielle. She had been following all the racing events in Puerto Rico since she left for college.

"A couple of years ago one of my friends from high school competed in the Cuomo race and was a near winner at one hour and twenty seconds. They were giving out $8,000 to the first woman who came in with a time under one hour and fourteen minutes. My friend Jane Rullán came in second place and won $5,000."

"I guess you can make a lot of money in these races, then!" responded Gabrielle.

"Oh, there's even a bigger race than that!"

Victoria continued to relate that in 1998 a retired U.S. Army colonel and San Juan businessman, Rafael Acosta, started a small 2.4 kilometer race to celebrate the opening of the San José Lagoon

Bridge. The race had been so popular with the locals that he decided to advertise it in the States. After a couple of years he began calling it the "World's Best 10-K," and it started gaining notoriety. Now it was attended by a field of about fourteen thousand internationally known runners, with a prize purse of about $500,000. Women were running as well and making a time of about thirty one minutes for the 6.2 mile race. Victoria knew about the race and had wanted to go to Puerto Rico a couple of years ago while she was training, but the accident got in her way. The race took place every February when it was a little cooler on the island. The temperatures typically hovered in the low 80's for the race, with the humidity in the low 70's. That was probably why this committee requesting Victoria's help would want to do the marathon in December.

"So tell me about this organization that is asking you to help them with the race" her friend asked. "Is it on the up-and-up?"

"Okay, let me look at this brochure that came with the letter. It's called *La Fundación de Cáncer y Salud de Puerto Rico, Inc.* It's an organization that started in the south of the island in 1945 to help improve the quality of life for patients with cancer. It says that their mission is to contribute to education, prevention and treatment of the disease. It looks like they have worked mostly in the south, east and west of the island, but they want to start organizing more fundraisers in the north. That's probably why they're looking at a marathon route in the northern part of the island."

"Vicky, you'd better go and do this or I will be very disappointed in you. This is your way to get back into the racing circuit! Since you can't compete, just think of the excitement of organizing your own race! So how much will they pay you? Will you be able to take the fall term off from teaching at the university? I wonder if there is a direct flight from Paris to Puerto Rico. What do you think I would need to bring to wear in December on the island?"

"Whoa, slow it down!" Victoria laughed. "Do you really think I can do it? I mean, I've only been a runner, not an organizer! And they're putting all their trust in me for this! No, it's too big, and Jennifer will be going off to college, and ..."

"Vicky," her friend responded, "you are supposed to do this. I don't know why, but I just have a feeling about it. Do it."

"Okay." She hesitated for a moment. "Okay!" she said more resolutely.

# CHAPTER EIGHTEEN

It was Monday, and it promised to be a very hectic week. The family was preparing for Christopher's graduation, and Jennifer was preparing for her final exams from high school before her own graduation two weeks later. Gabrielle was planning on staying through the following weekend so that she could attend the one graduation; then leave for New York for a week to meet with some designers, and then she'd be back or Jennifer's graduation.

Rebecca would be coming in on Thursday afternoon and would spend the night so that she could join the rest of the family headed to James Madison University on Friday. Christopher's graduation was on Saturday, and she wasn't going to miss her first grandchild's graduation!

Victoria had talked to Christopher about his thoughts regarding the marathon. She hadn't mentioned it to Jennifer, because she had wanted her daughter to concentrate on her final exams. Christopher was all in favor and was ready to help with whatever she needed. They discussed how this might be a business opportunity for him as well.

During the week Victoria consulted with the university where she taught, and she was assured that she would likely be granted leave of absence without pay for the fall term, and then be reinstated for the second semester. She had been doing some research for Johns Hopkins University that year, and they agreed that she could continue the research project by telecommuting while she was in Puerto Rico. She really didn't need to take off all that time, but she was almost grateful for the semester of leave. It was time for a break. She knew she would be paid for being the race director, so that would be sufficient for bills and any of Jennifer's college expenses for the first semester. Jennifer had already received the news about the scholarship to UVA, so the costs would be minimal.

Victoria wondered what she would do about Jennifer in the summer if she had to go to Puerto Rico often. Jennifer could probably stay with Tom, or maybe even come with her on some of the trips. Victoria figured that she wouldn't really be gone all summer, because there would be a lot of things for the race that she could work on from her home in Maryland.

If she were to accept this venture, where on earth would she begin? She started a list. The date and time for the race had already been determined by the committee that enlisted her help. They probably already had a name picked out for the race as well. She'd have to map out the course and have it certified by the International Association of Athletics Foundations. The ideas started to bombard her mind and she quickly wrote them down so as not to forget. Design a race form and waiver. Maybe the race form should have a way to raise pledges like the Leukemia Teams in Maryland. They would certainly need bank accounts and accountants for all of this. A confirmation card that will be sent to applicants. Someone to be in charge of flyer distribution and advertising; the press. Road insurance, road signs, and police assistance. Paint, yellow tape, and cones. Clocks, split timers, computer operations, data entry, timing and results books. Contact ChampionChip for an online timing system. Marshalls and volunteers. Aid stations and medics, and decisions as to where they would be placed. Security and race officials. Sound and light. Bag check areas. Maps for participants and their families who will be asking where to go to watch the race. Food to distribute to runners after the race. Some token for all the runners like a Puerto Rican coquí keychain? T-shirts. Sponsors and plenty of donations for prizes. Trophies and medals. Contact and invite some *rabbits*, the people who would be pacing and leading the elite runners. Hotels and flight information for participants. Packets with bib numbers, pins, instructions and course maps, and then places to pick up the packets a few days in advance or maybe even a week in advance. Volunteers to manage the registration. A dinner for the volunteers? Lead bike, lead vehicles, and a car to bring up the rear. Photography for sure. People always liked to buy pictures of themselves running. Running clinics several days before the marathon; speakers for the clinics. Water stops, jugs for the water, cups, tables, sports drinks and sports bars. Pens. Posters. A website for sure! Gosh, what about an aerobics-type person to do the warm-up right before the race? An announcer; maybe the Mayor of San Juan? What about a wheelchair race? A fun run to begin the race? Shit, what if it *rained*?!

The list was getting longer. Victoria was wondering what on earth she was getting herself into. But it was exciting. It would mean a lot of hard work, but she wasn't afraid of hard work, and she had been promised a good workforce.

Maybe Rina could help with advertising advice. Christopher would be getting his athletic business off the ground, too, and this would be the perfect opportunity for him to advertise his athletic clothing line, perhaps serve as a sponsor, and maybe even sell some stuff at the pre-race conference day. Speaking of Christopher …

"Hello, Chris?" asked his mom with the phone receiver in one hand and her list and pen in the other.

"Hi, mom!"

"Hi, honey. Listen," she said to her son "we'll be arriving in Harrisonburg on Friday afternoon, and we'd like to get together for dinner if you don't have a bunch of graduation things to do. What do you think? Great! About 5:30pm? Can you pick out a place and make a reservation? No, goofy, a nice restaurant! No peanut butter and jelly sandwiches! Okay, so I guess there will be about five of us: you, me, Jen, grandma, and Gabrielle. Aunt Rina and Rob will be coming on Saturday morning. I think your dad is still planning on coming down on Saturday morning too, right? And who? Adam will be there?" Her heart skipped a beat.

Chris explained that Adam had twin cousins who also attended the James Madison, and they were graduating with this class as well. Adam was going to come down early on Friday. His family wasn't going to come down until Saturday, so Chris had invited Adam to dinner with them on Friday.

After hanging up, Victoria's mind was not on the graduation plans or on the race. All she could think about was what her son had said: that Adam was coming to the graduation. After all, Adam and Christopher were kind of friends. It was her fault for introducing them to each other years ago when she was in the hospital recuperating from the accident. Dan had come to see her that one day in the hospital, and he had brought Adam along with him so that it would look safe. He had wanted Victoria to meet Adam, so they told the children that Dan had been one of her coaches helping to train her for the Olympic trials. It had seemed harmless enough, and in a sense it was true. They had encouraged the friendship when the boys were in their last year of high school, because it had given them a chance to see each other when either he or she would drop their sons off at each others' houses. She just didn't realize that they had stayed in touch as much, and that he would be at Chris' graduation! Victoria actually liked Adam. It was his father Dan that she did not want to see. Surely his father wouldn't be coming back for his nieces' graduation. Would he? God, she prayed that Dan was still in Arizona.

The conversations with Gabrielle about the whole affair had been liberating. Victoria felt like she could finally put the whole thing behind her and look forward to an exciting future. It didn't matter that she had messed up in a relationship. Again. Who cared? And it wasn't important anymore that she had fallen in love and her heart had been broken. Big deal. She just didn't want to have to relive the whole thing again. She hoped that she could look at Adam and not see his father.

# CHAPTER NINETEEN

The trip to Harrisonburg had been uneventful and they arrived right on schedule. Christopher called Victoria at her hotel room from his apartment, and they were all set for dinner at the designated time.

"Mom, you remember Adam, right?" Chris asked as they entered the restaurant later that evening.

"Of course I do! Congratulations on your own graduation from the University of Arizona, Adam."

"Thank you" he responded as everyone hugged and said their hellos.

As they waited for their food to be served, everyone talked incessantly, with the topic changing so rapidly, that Victoria had trouble keeping up! It warmed her heart to have all the family together, and she was so proud of her son and all his accomplishments. He had turned into such a nice young man. He was respectful, intelligent, responsible, and very self-motivated. She knew she wouldn't have to worry about him at all after graduation, even given the state of the economy and the difficulty with unemployment. Christopher had all his plans set up, and everything was falling into place for him. Life couldn't get much better than this, she thought.

"Adam, Chris tells me that you are looking at graduate schools here in Virginia and in Maryland, is that right?" Victoria asked.

"Well," he answered, "if I pass the Law School Admission Test in June, I'll be going to law school at the University of Arizona, and I've already been accepted pending my scores since I went there for my undergrad. But if I don't pass, I'll come back east and go to graduate school here. I'm pretty sure I'll be going to law school, though. I had tried to take the test in February, but I got food poisoning and was in the hospital for three days, so the next administration is in June."

"Great! So will you be able to stay in Maryland this summer with your mom before returning?"

"Actually, I'll be here for about two weeks, and then I'm going back. My dad and I met this old guy up in Oracle who lives in the mountains. We worked with him and a group of people last summer clearing parts of the Arizona Trail, so we're going to go back and help some more with some other projects."

That caught Jennifer's attention, because she loved horses and mountains.

"How long is the trail?" Jennifer asked.

"About 750 miles that extends from New Mexico to Canada. It should be completed soon, so we're all going to ride part of it with this guy and help him with checkpoints to change horses, get food, and so forth. Want to come?!" He was teasing, of course.

"I wish!" responded Jennifer. "So your dad is going to do it too?"

"He'll participate in part of it, but he's more of a runner than a cowboy! You can ask him yourself, though, because he'll be here tomorrow. He's coming with the rest of my family for my cousins' graduation, Melissa and Allie."

Jennifer continued asking Adam a multitude of questions about cowboys and horses, the ranch they stayed on, and mountain lions. Victoria pretended she was listening, but she felt numb after hearing that Dan would be at the graduation the next day. The voices around her disappeared into the background. No one seemed to notice except Gabrielle. And maybe Christopher.

"Vicky, can you show me where the restroom is?" urged Gabrielle.

"Oh, sure," she answered, somewhat dazed.

"Let's go outside," Gabrielle whispered as they walked away from the table.

"Gabi, what am I going to do?!" The tears started to form in Victoria's eyes.

"Nothing, Vicky. Nothing," she responded as she put both hands on Victoria's shoulders and looked her straight in the eyes. "Look at me. You will just be yourself. You are in control, you know. You didn't do anything. You owe him nothing. He doesn't hate you, he isn't coming back to try to win you over."

"But he should hate me! I never answered his calls or his letters. Maybe he had a perfectly good explanation for being with *Miss Brunette*, and I never listened. I just felt like it was the final blow in a relationship that wasn't working. Do you think he figured that out? God, I'm being so melodramatic, aren't I?" She laughed through tears.

"A bit, maybe!" her friend laughed with her.

"Okay, so what do I say when I see him?" Victoria said wiping her eyes and composing herself.

"You just say hello. That's it. Life goes on."

Victoria smiled at her friend. "Okay, you're right. *Hello*. And that's it, right?"

"Just be normal. Ask him how he's doing. Like seeing an old friend. Ask about Arizona."

"But he's not just an old friend, Gabi. You know, I never felt like anything was for keeps when I was young; like God would take it away like Esperanza and my step-dad. I think that just stuck with me. Too much moving around, losing ones you loved. Then when I started dating, I guess I just always braced myself for loss and breakups, so I'd never allow myself to be completely attached. Until Dan. I forgot to brace myself. Whew. I just don't want to see him or think about him anymore. I just want to move on."

"Do you think that he is here to see you?"

"Well what else could it be? I mean, come on, he's in Harrisonburg to go to his nieces' graduation, and my son just happens to be graduating from the same place on the same day?"

"Mom?" Christopher had walked up behind them. Victoria

quickly wiped the last of her tears and smiled. This was Chris' dinner; *his* time.

"Hi, sweetie!" She blew her nose into a tissue. "I guess I'm just weepy about your graduation and all. You and Jennifer are just so grown up all of a sudden! What do they call it? I'm having *empty nest* feelings?" She laughed.

Chris laughed too and hugged his mom. "Aunt Gabrielle, do you think I can have a few minutes with my mom?"

"Of course!" she responded and patted him on the shoulder as she left.

"Mom, I know this is about Adam's father."

"What?" She looked at him stunned.

"The story Jennifer found. The man with the brown jacket was Dan."

"How did you---"

"The pilot wings on the jacket. It's okay, you know. He's a good man."

Victoria grabbed him and just hugged him. Her son was so mature.

"I know it's about Jen and me too! I know you're proud of us, and you should be!" he said humorously. They both laughed and then walked back to the table.

⚜⚜⚜⚜⚜

The graduates walked in after their professors, the president of the university, various officials, and the keynote speaker. The place was packed. Cameras flashed from every corner.

Dan walked up behind Victoria and tapped her on the shoulder just as he had years before when they had first met on the track. She turned around and gasped. She didn't want this to ruin the graduation for her, and she knew what to do.

"Hello," she said.

"Hello," he responded. She missed his voice. She wondered

what he was thinking. She wanted to know why he had let her walk away. But that was a conversation for another time, not now.

"Vicky," Tom walked up to them. "Where are we sitting?"

"Right up there on the third row. You see Jennifer and Rina up there where I'm pointing?" she answered as calmly as she could.

"Well," said Dan looking at his watch, "I'd better let you get to your seat because it looks like they'll be starting in a few minutes." He walked the other way and sat with Adam on the opposite side.

Following the ceremony, the family met out on the lawn and waited as Christopher said his goodbyes to his classmates and exchanged phone numbers and email addresses. Victoria searched the crowd for a glimpse of Dan. He was standing near a tree with his hands in his pockets laughing and listening to Adam and Jennifer talk. Victoria started walking toward them and then stopped suddenly. Another woman was walking up to Dan. The woman linked her arm through his and whispered in his ear making him smile and kiss her on the cheek. Jennifer waved goodbye to Adam and walked up the hill to her mother.

"Hi, mom! Everything okay?" she asked.

"Everything is fine."

# CHAPTER TWENTY

Victoria spent the summer tying up loose ends at the university and getting together some data for the research she was going to do for Hopkins while on leave. She'd work on that while doing whatever it is that race directors do. Right now, however, she needed to fly down to Puerto Rico to meet the race committee and sponsors to get the ball rolling.

"I think you're sitting in my seat," she said to the man on Air Tran in 21-C.

"Oh, I'm sorry." He moved to the next seat over. "Can I keep my bag under your seat, though? It won't fit under this middle one."

"Sure."

Victoria wasn't too happy about this, because it meant that she had to put her own bag in the baggage compartment above. She tried stuffing it into the closest compartment even though it was pretty much full, and the bag fell out twice. The man who had been in her seat made no attempt to help her at all. He just continued typing on his laptop. She was so irritated at that point that she punched the bag and shoved it in as hard as she could and slammed the door. She hoped that nothing had broken in the bag, and if it had, she would sue the man in 21-B!

The aircraft took off without incident. After eating the lunch she had brought along with her, she decided to read one of the books she had packed for her research project. But of course, the book was in the bag above in the small cramped compartment. She slipped out of her seat and into the aisle. As soon as she clicked open the overhead compartment, her stuffed backpack came crashing down onto Mr. 21-B and spilled his drink all over the computer on his lap.

"Oh, gosh, I'm so sorry!" She really was sorry. As irritated as she had been about not being able to use her space under her seat so that he could accommodate *his* bag, she still would not have wished this on anyone. Laptops are not cheap, and a spilled soda could mean the end for even the best computer.

The passenger in 21-B had jumped out of his seat dangling the laptop in both hands trying to shake off the liquid.

"Not good," he said a bit annoyed, but not overwhelmingly so.

The steward helped him clean up the mess. His seat was soaking wet.

"Poetic justice'" she whispered under her breath, not sure whether she really meant it.

"What?" he asked.

"Your pants," she quickly said. "Your pants are all wet." Duh. What a stupid thing to say, she thought. But 21-B just laughed, and she was relieved.

"Don't worry, he said. Accidents happen." The steward motioned him over to a dry seat a couple of rows away.

"I really am sorry about the computer," she went back to tell him.

"It's okay. It belongs to my company. It's replaceable. I'm just trying to get what I was working on. Hopefully it didn't affect the flashdrive."

She went back to her seat and opened her backpack to get the book. The three ounce bottle of apricot shampoo had spilled all over the other contents in her bag. In the bag, of course, was her mini laptop. She just closed the backpack and laid her head on the headrest.

"Not good," she said.

# CHAPTER TWENTY-ONE

Victoria was met by an airport shuttle in Isla Verde that took her to the Rio Mar Beach Hotel about half an hour away. The hotel was located on the northeast coast of the island, with the tropical rainforest El Yunque about fifteen minutes to the south. The island was still breathtaking, she contemplated along the way as she looked out the window of the shuttle. Lush green. Flowers in reds and pinks and yellows everywhere. Humid. Very humid. Gorgeous brown bodies walking along the roads. The sounds were different and the smells were different from the mainland. Welcome home, she thought. Welcome home. Today I begin a new life.

After unpacking her bags, Victoria put on her running shoes and went down to the lobby of the hotel, out the main entrance, and onto the street for a run. She had never explored this area because she didn't even remember this hotel existing when she grew up on the island. So much had changed! And yet, there was much that was still the same. People still greeted her with friendly remarks as she ran by. She loved the sounds and beats of the Latino music coming from open doors, the lace curtains blowing in the gentle breeze, and the smells of rice and beans permeating the air. She had run easily forty minutes before she realized she had better turn around, or she wouldn't make it back up the steep hill to the hotel in time for her first meeting!

Victoria had been running sporadically since her accident, but never more than six to eight miles on a long run, and certainly never for speed. She felt strong, and her hip was agreeable to these shorter runs as long as she took it easy. She barely had a trace of a limp. Her shoulder did hurt at times during the cold winters, but it had healed well. All in all, she considered herself very lucky to have made it through as well as she did after the awful accident that took away her ability to run competitively. And still, here she was right in the center of all the excitement of racing again; just in a different capacity.

After finishing her run, Victoria walked through the lobby on Italian tile floors and sat down on a large stuffed tan sofa. She looked around. The lobby was decorated with muted green colors, ambers, and pastel shades of lemon and blue. To her left was a long dark mahogany bar where a few guests sat and listened to a piano player who was playing soft jazz on a grand piano nearby. She could see across from her a view of the beach through the large glass windows that hung from the ceiling all the way to the floor. There were green trees growing everywhere in rich clay pots painted with Taino Indian symbols. The walls were adorned with beautiful paintings of the Caribbean Sea and the rainforest.

"Victoria Taylor?" asked a tall woman with long dark hair and a heavy accent.

"Yes."

"Welcome to the Rio Mar. Margaret Santos." They shook hands. "I'm one of the hotel managers. I've been asked to remind you that the meeting with the Board of Directors and race committee will meet at five o'clock in the lobby, and then a dinner and show will follow in the restaurant."

"Thank you so much!"

"Please let me know if there is anything I can do to help you while you stay with us at the Rio Mar."

Yes, thought Victoria. She wanted to ask how this woman got her gorgeous tan.

She looked at her watch. Four thirty. How did that happen?! And how did this Ms. Santos even know who she was, anyway? Probably the running clothes. What other fool would come to a paradise like this and run away from it as soon as she arrived? She raced up the stairs to the next floor to get a shower.

At five o'clock, and smelling very much like the apricot

shampoo that had spilled all over everything in her bag, Victoria entered the lobby and was greeted by the Director of Catering and Conference Services, Mr. Honorio Hernández. She had been told ahead of time that he would be handling the conference services for the group. He was fabulous at his job. He explained to Victoria that the hotel had 75,000 square feet of conference facilities and meeting rooms, and that he would be glad to show her committee the two ballrooms if they chose to use those for their pre-race symposiums and packet pick-up locations. Then he made sure all the committee members got to the designated room reserved just for them at the restaurant, that they all had drinks, and that they all had whatever supplies they needed for the meeting that evening. As a matter of fact, he took care of their every whim for the remainder of their stay at the hotel.

Everything looked so impressive. Her eyes scanned the room. All of these people were counting on her as the race director to bring the meeting to order and welcome them all there. *Oh God*, all these people were working for *her*! Victoria felt a wave of nerves. She opened her leather binder to look at her notes one more time. Okay, so the major sponsors should be here. The presenting sponsors, which were the bank and the printing company, should also be here. Did they have any platinum or gold sponsors yet? Were the assistant race directors here? Which one was her deputy race director, this Bryan Villanueva guy?

"Shall we get started?" someone had asked from the crowd. Victoria headed for an inconspicuous seat towards the middle or the table, but Mr. Hernández quickly indicated that she was to sit at the head of the table with the director of the hotel, since the hotel was also a major sponsor of the event.

The introductions began, and Victoria tried hard to remember names and titles without foolishly writing them down. There was a city planner, several hotel officials, assistant race directors for logistics, registration, promotion, volunteers, course operations, safety, start and finish line operations, results, and---

"Sorry I'm late," she heard a voice say as she looked up from her notes.

"Oh, good," said Mario, the director of the hotel. He turned to Victoria. "This is our deputy race director and treasurer, Bryan Villanueva. Bryan, this is Victoria Taylor, the director of this marathon."

Suddenly the smell of apricot shampoo was overwhelming. The two people stood and stared at each other.

"Yes," said Bryan, "we met on the plane. Sorry I'm late. I had to replace my laptop." He smiled at her, and she grew red in the face.

The preliminary meeting went well, and the dinner was exquisite. The hotel restaurant faced walls of glass that looked out onto the beach, and the moon and stars shone down on the tables from skylights above. The tables were covered with pink linens and the china had a pink and turquoise rim to match. There were pink orchids at every table. The service was outstanding, very unobtrusive and polite. After dinner the guests watched a superb performance of the Ballet Folklórico.

"Can I show you around the premises?" Bryan asked as he leaned in to Victoria while the dancers were finishing their bows.

"Well, it's late," answered Victoria, "and we have a busy day tomorrow."

"There's a mean grass hut down on the beach where Ramón makes the quintessential piña colada!"

Victoria sighed.

"One?" he urged holding up one finger.

The beach was beautiful at night. Victoria hadn't realized during the day how loudly the waves crash before resting on the sand. Ramón's hut was well lit with sparkling lights. Bryan was right; the piña colada surpassed any she had ever had. After all, the drink was said to have been invented in Puerto Rico! Ramón was a real character. He had a quick wit and could dish back anything thrown to him with a twist that left you laughing. He had been working at the hotel since it had opened. He was a little rotund, a little bald, and a lot brown. Victoria knew they were going to be fast friends.

"Listen, I'm sorry about the pants and your laptop," Victoria apologized again.

"Don't even worry about it! I don't like wearing dress pants anyway! I'm more of a beach bum type to tell you the truth."

Victoria figured that Bryan was a little younger than she, and she learned that he lived in Northern Virginia when not travelling for work. He worked for a digital network company and was selected to help with the race because of his expertise in computer operations. And he was a runner. And he spoke Spanish fluently. He was single, she noted, but she was not quite sure if that was good or bad.

Bryan asked how Victoria had been chosen to help with the race, and she told him in loose detail about her running career.

"Bryan, I'm still curious about how they selected you, of all computer geeks around, to help with this race. No offense, certainly, but there are plenty of well qualified people right here on the island!"

"Mario, the director of the hotel, is my brother," he responded with a smile.

"Wow! Okay, that makes sense! Mario Villanueva."

"It's getting late and I promised to get you back after one drink," he said. "Come on, I'll walk you to your room and tell you about the hotel as we go along. I could probably answer any question you have about it, because I've spent so much time here!"

Victoria learned that the hotel was actually considered a golf resort and spa, and that it was renovated from a structure that previously belonged to the Spaniards. Bryan explained that they have about six hundred guest rooms and suites, eleven restaurants, two 18-hole golf courses, and twelve certified tennis courts. She couldn't wait to explore all the running trails, and then start making plans for the marathon event that would start right there at the Rio Mar Hotel!

# CHAPTER TWENTY-TWO

The phone rang loudly next to the bed stand the next morning.
"Hello?"

"This is your wake-up call as requested, Ms. Taylor."

"Oh yes, thank you." Victoria replaced the receiver and rolled over to stare out the window beyond the balcony surrounded by clear blue sky.

She lazily got up and put on some running clothes. *What a gorgeous morning,* she thought, as she ran through the streets away from the hotel. As she ran, she tried to imagine what the marathon runners would think about the course. Flowers bloomed everywhere, and they would still be blooming in December. She noticed that chickens and iguanas still roamed freely about, so she would have to warn the runners about the critters. It started to get hot and muggy, but it should only be in the low 70's for the race. She wouldn't have to worry about heat stroke for the runners. Dehydration, yes. She hoped that runners from the colder climates would consider the acclimatization factors and build their tolerance for running in the warmer weather even though it would be in the winter.

"Hey, stranger!"

It was Bryan. What was he doing out here on *her* road? Of course, he was running on *his* road. There had been only two choices from the hotel: run west or run east, unless one ran north and plunked into the sea or south into the rainforest. She had gone east. Less populated, less pollution, yet more chickens in the road. Apparently he had figured that out too.

"Turn back!" he said.

"Why?!" How dare he tell her, an expert runner, to turn back!

"You're five miles out from the hotel!"

He had remembered her conversation from the previous night when she recounted the events that led to her retirement from competitive distance running. *Holy Toledo,* she thought, *five miles out!* He caught up with her and they turned around.

Victoria struggled to keep up with Bryan, so she let him do all the talking on the way back. He was actually a pleasant conversationalist. But she still couldn't figure out if he was a ladies' man or really just a nice person. He was certainly very handsome with his tall slender body and longish blonde hair and brown eyes. He was smart and had a good job and was probably earning a good salary. So why was he single? What was the catch?

"Water!" he gasped with his tongue hanging out as they neared the hotel entrance.

"You are such a fake!" she accused.

He went straight to the water fountain at the main entrance, took off his shoes, and jumped in! Victoria yelled for him to get out, but he reached over and grabbed her arm to pull her in.

"*Socorro!*" she yelled and laughed outright.

"May I help you out, Sir?" came the question from one of the managers who had just been summoned by another employee.

"Yes, thank you," he said. "I seem to have fallen in. Heat exhaustion. Dizziness, you know."

Victoria and Bryan both ran quickly up to the lobby laughing. He dripped across the floor all the way to the elevators.

"Meetings all morning, it looks like. See you at lunch?" he asked.

"Sure." *Sure,* she thought. *Why not?*

The Steering Committee was very serious. And so was Victoria. They knew that they had to come up with some scheme that would attract runners to the marathon. They were competing with another major marathon scheduled for January at Disney

World in Florida. It seemed crazy to schedule this one so closely. But the summer months were so hot, and no one would want to travel to the Caribbean in the fall. In the spring there was the Boston Marathon. They needed an attraction, a gimmick.

"What about a festival?" asked one of the deputies. "Puerto Rico is known for its festivals and carnivals all year long. We have more holidays than there are days in the year!"

"Not a bad idea," said another member of the team. "We could have a festival the evening after the race. Roast some pigs and eat *lechón*, display some arts and crafts sold by our local artists; do some dancing, and have some *carrozas*."

"*Carrozas?*" whispered an American to one of the members.

"Floats," she whispered back.

"What about a big beach party?" one of the member's asked.

"Drowning," replied another. "We don't want to read about it in the papers."

"A big party at the town square in Old San Juan?"

"Oh, I know! A party at the fortress of El Morro!"

"Yeah, and then someone will fall off one of the walls and crash into the rocks in the water, and its dinner time for the *tiburones!*"

"Safety, people! If there is drinking and dancing, there has to be safety!"

"So I guess the mountainside chairlift at *El Conquistador* is out, right?"

People laughed and someone threw an empty plastic water bottle at the person making the comment.

Bryan passed a note to Victoria. '*Ever been on a Catamaran?*' it said.

Victoria turned towards him and shook her head no.

He motioned to his watch and mouthed the words '*meet me at lunch.*'

*This man is definitely too young for me* she thought. But maybe she was reading too much into it. They were working buddies, right? Surely he wasn't interested in anything else.

"Okay, people," she heard herself saying. "Let's get back to the idea about the carnival."

Bryan sequestered Victoria when the group broke for lunch. They wouldn't be meeting for another couple of hours, so there would be plenty of time for lunch and whatever this *Catamaran* idea was of his.

"Come on!" he said grabbing her by the hand. "Go get your bathing suit!"

Bryan took her to the diving shop on the premises and checked out some snorkeling equipment from one of the guys at the desk. Victoria wondered if they didn't need to make a reservation for the water activities at the hotel, but Bryan seemed to know everyone and they seemed eager to please him. Victoria figured by the equipment that they were going on a snorkeling adventure. They joined two other couples and an instructor for a sailing adventure on a beautiful Catamaran; okay, a *boat*. A *big* boat. Victoria had seen these in all the travel magazines, but had never had the money or opportunity to enjoy one of these types of adventures. They sailed along the Puerto Rican coastline and marveled at the views of El Yunque, a 28,000 acre tropical rainforest; the only one of its kind in the US National Forest system. The instructor or tour guide on the boat explained that El Yunque is at the top elevations of the eastern side of the Luquillo Mountains, and that it rains there most of the time as the breezes hit the mountain and convert to water as they rise.

The boat sailed its way through some very small deserted islands, and the guests finally stopped at one of them to eat a buffet lunch the instructors had brought along.

"Okay, time for some snorkeling," said Bryan. "Have you ever been?"

"No," she responded, "I lived here for so long, but snorkeling is something I missed. What do I do?"

"Don't worry, the instructor will tell you everything. Just don't touch anything on the reefs and don't walk on them, okay?"

"What do you mean?" she asked.

"The reefs are deteriorating, so we want to protect them."

Bryan got the instructor to take them out snorkeling on the reef, and Victoria saw some amazing water creatures that she hadn't even know existed! There were hues of pink, orange, auburn and green on the reefs as they got further out, but closer in there were splotches on the coral, and it looked hard and bleached. She asked the instructor about it after they had surfaced.

"Puerto Rico is surrounded by coral ecosystems," he explained, "but high population density and coastal construction have had a bad impact. What you saw that was bleached-looking was the coral that is dying."

"What do you mean?"

"The coral is made up of tiny animals, about 1,500 species, and they live in colonies and feed at night on microscopic plants and creatures. So the coral's surface that you were seeing is the living part. Unfortunately, scientists are saying that human factors are to blame for the deterioration of coral around the world. Others disagree and say it is the change in water temperatures and current patterns, like what happened after El Niño, the hurricane in 1998. But there are really a lot more possible reasons."

"So what will happen if it all dies?" she asked quite astonished and genuinely interested.

"Well, they estimate that corals are worth about $300-400 billion each year to the economy, so that would be a big loss for many people."

"Wow! In what way? I mean, how does it benefit the economy?" She was amazed. She had never thought much about coral.

"Fishing, tourism, other industries."

"So what is being done about it?" She hoped she wasn't

appearing too ignorant by all the questions.

"There is an organization sponsored by the Congress on the mainland that is researching and monitoring the situation. We know that the corals still spawn once a year, so we are hopeful they will regenerate."

As they walked from the water up to the beach to join the others, Victoria was excited about this new information. Jennifer had been talking about studying marine biology at one point, even though Victoria doubted that UVA had a degree in that field. But who knows? Maybe she could go to Florida for a graduate degree? It would be great if Jennifer joined the research team in the islands to protect these beautiful reefs!

As they sat on the beach, Victoria asked Bryan why he had an English name while his brother had a Spanish name.

"My parents came from wealthy families in Chile. They met, got married, tried for years to have kids, and ended up adopting Mario. Later they moved to the States and found me."

"Found you?" she asked.

"My father is a pediatrician. Someone brought me to the hospital one night and just left me there. And here I am!"

"I'm sorry," she said sympathetically.

"I'm not. I'm very lucky, actually."

"So you are actually an American."

Yes, by birth I am an American."

It was time to go back. In the course of the conversation, Victoria had learned that Bryan was actually five years younger than she. This surprised her, because he seemed so much older. But actually, it was good to find out now rather than later, so that she wouldn't even think about developing a crush on him. She had always told herself that she would never go out with a younger man. She liked men who were a little older than herself, a little wiser, and who would maybe take care of her instead of her having to take care of them. It was just as well that Bryan was off limits, in her mind, because it is never wise to get involved romantically with someone with whom you have to work.

She also learned that he wasn't as spoiled as she thought he should be for a person who comes from a family of wealth. He was bright. He had attended Harvard and later the London School of Economics for one year. He eventually settled for a job in a large company in Northern Virginia because he loved going to the performances at the Kennedy Center and at Wolf Trap, or so he said. She later found out that he had actually fallen in love with a resident at Georgetown Hospital, but she never found out why they didn't get married. It wasn't appropriate to ask, and he didn't volunteer the information.

# CHAPTER TWENTY-THREE

"Okay, let's quiet down!" Victoria addressed the members of the committee.

"So we agree that we will have the start and finish for the race at this hotel just at the bottom of the hill on the golf course, right?" she asked.

"And then we will have the awards ceremony just at four hours after the start time," she continued, "because our top runners should be coming in at about two and a half hours. Then we close the race at five hours, and fiesta afterwards. Agreed?"

"Victoria, can't we make this a people's race and include all runners regardless of time? Do we have to be so elitist? I mean, after all, this is a fundraiser!" commented the registration and promotion chair.

"Good question! Let me ask you this first: are we going to cap the race?"

"I say no," added the woman in charge of inviting the top athletes.

There were numerous nods around the table indicating agreement.

"Okay, statistics man, what do you think we're looking at size-wise if we don't restrict entries?" Victoria asked Bryan.

"I think for our first race, four or five thousand would be a fair estimate," he answered. "Boston is usually about ten thousand and closes at five hours. The Marine Corps Marathon in Washington closes at six hours and draws about fifteen thousand."

"That's a lot of water cups!" remarked one of the members and they all laughed.

"Okay," Victoria said, "so let's say we have an open race without qualification times, closing the race at six hours, and hoping to attract at least three thousand runners. That would eliminate investigating all the qualifying times for the November first deadline."

"Let's add a half-marathon," the promotion chair ventured further. "Disney added one to their marathon, and they had a larger draw."

"Well?" Victoria addressed the group. She liked the idea. They all agreed and began talking about how this would improve their chances of a larger field of entrants.

'*Meet me at the fountain at 5 o'clock before dinner*' read the note that Bryan now pushed in front of Victoria. She turned and nodded once again. She wondered what the adventure would be this time.

"Okay," she addressed the group, "this is our last day here, so let's go over this list one more time to confirm everyone's responsibilities. Remember, your team captains report to you, you report to Bryan, and he reports to me. We meet again in one month."

Did she sound too demanding, she wondered? No, she thought, that's what they are paying her for; to organize this race. She proceeded to read off the list for each assistant race director. They made some changes and added some new tasks resulting from the addition of the half-marathon.

They finished the meeting by addressing the concern about race bandits and cheaters. Cheaters were the runners who missed the registration deadline or hadn't paid the entry fee and they'd run without numbers. That always screwed up the finish line statistics. They'd be clocked, but wouldn't have a number to turn in. *Race bandits*, as they were called, were different than the cheaters, but even worse. They were runners who would show up in the larger races where the purse money for the winners was a large sum. They'd start the marathon with all the other runners, then veer off inconspicuously during the race, cover a good bit of distance by car, and join the race for the last five or six miles. Some of those bandits had even been declared big prize winners in their age groups in some major races. One suspicious race commissioner, however, decided to videotape his race at crucial checkpoints. When he viewed the videotapes after the race, and after the prize money had been distributed, he couldn't find the winning racer anywhere at the midpoint or thirteen mile marker. The contestant had to return the money and was humiliated. Apparently the racer had hopped on a train to cover some of the distance and then joined the race without anyone being the wiser! Then all major races began hiring videographers. Race commissioners started exposing these frauds publicly as a deterrent. Their names were splashed across TV screens and in running magazines. *What an insult to the running profession*, she thought. Eventually tracking tags, or micro-chips attached to the runner's shoe, replaced the videotaping. They were more accurate. The contestants would receive a micro-chip that would be tied to the shoelaces of one shoe, and then at specific points in the race, they would run over mats that would electronically track where they were and what their running time had been at that point. No one knew in advance where the mats would be placed in the races, so they would have to run the full course to make sure they crossed each matt.

# CHAPTER TWENTY-FOUR

"You are a very punctual person," Bryan said to Victoria as he looked at his watch. "Five o'clock on the dot!"

Bryan was dressed handsomely in navy slacks and a yellow button down shirt. Victoria had tried on and discarded four dresses before settling on a silk blue dress with cream colored sandals.

"Our carriage is waiting. Are you ready?" He pointed to a golf cart near one of the hotel attendants. The employee shrugged his shoulders and smiled.

After escorting Victoria to the cart, Bryan climbed into the driver's seat. He leaned over to the back of the cart and pulled out a bottle of champagne. The attendant quickly motioned that he would be honored to open it, and he did so without having the cork fly wildly in the air. He must have radioed ahead, because at that precise moment, another attendant arrived with two champagne flutes.

"To a job well-done," said Bryan as he raised his glass.

"To a job well-done," repeated Victoria.

They left the attendants to their smiles as they rode off into the sunset. Well, that's what it had seemed like, but it was still too early for the sun to set.

"Where are we going?" asked Victoria.

"Up," he responded.

And so they did. Bryan drove the golf cart down the road a bit past the golf course, turned to the right, and continued driving up a long winding hill to the top until they arrived at a beautiful restaurant at the edge of the cliff called *Richie's Bar and Restaurant*. It was lit up with sparkling lights and had blossoming orange flowers hanging from the balcony overlooking the cliff and spilling out towards the beach far below. Bryan put his arm around

Victoria and escorted her into the restaurant.

They sat out on the balcony and ordered wine as they gazed out to the sea and watched the sun slowly descend into the water. The colors left behind were indescribable, and perhaps could only have been captured by an artist like El Greco, because the hues were so different than anything Victoria had ever seen. Was she really seeing greens and yellows in the sky?

Bryan ordered crab stuffed *tostones*, or plantains, for their appetizer. Then the owner came over to greet him and suggested the fillet of grouper topped with shrimp and creole sauce.

After dinner and the ride home, as if it couldn't have gotten any better, it did. They decided to visit Ramón's hut on the beach for one last drink; for old time's sake. *For old time's sake?* Victoria had only known Bryan for one week!

After the glass of wine, they walked along the beach barefooted and talked about their jobs and their hopes for the future. Nothing serious, though. No big revelations.

Neither talked about previous relationships. They almost instinctively knew that they were both here on this venture to heal from something, or someone.

Suddenly Bryan turned Victoria to face him and he gently pulled her into his arms. His hug was warm, and Victoria felt secure enveloped in his arms. The water was serene, and all she could hear was the distant sounds of laughter emanating from Ramón's hut further down the beach. He kissed the top of her head.

"Victoria, this really isn't like me," he hesitated, "and I know it isn't like you. But I want you to spend the night with me."

She did.

# CHAPTER TWENTY-FIVE

The next afternoon on the plane back to Maryland, Victoria sat by the window in deep thought. She watched the island disappear as the aircraft lifted its nose further into the sky. She turned and looked at the man sitting next to her.

"Bryan?"

"Yes?"

"I want to run," she said.

"You can't, Victoria," he laughed, "we are currently over a *big* water in a jet!"

"No, I mean, I want to run the marathon."

"No!"

"I do. I want to run," she declared.

"Victoria, please. You can't log one hundred mile weeks to train for this like you used to do. You'll get hurt." He gently kissed her hand.

"Just half, Bryan. The half-marathon. And I won't do it for speed."

"Why, Victoria? Why do you feel like you have to do this?"

"Because it's there," she said as she looked into the distance from the small window on the plane. "Because it's there."

Victoria arrived at the Baltimore International Airport late that evening. Bryan accompanied her to the shuttle and then left in another for Virginia. He had decided not to fly into Dulles airport, which would have been closer to home for him, so that he could spend more time with Victoria, even if it was on an airplane. It was difficult saying goodbye because they both knew intuitively that they may not see each other too much other than the times they had to meet with the committee to discuss the race. She had her life, and he had his. They lived about an hour apart from each other, they both had jobs, she had children, and the list of excuses went on.

Bryan was different, Victoria reflected, not like Tom and not like Dan. Although he was younger than she, and this certainly bothered her, he was one of the most grounded people she had known. They seemed on the surface, without really knowing each other too well, to have a lot in common. They shared a love for the outdoors, for wineries, classical movies and Asian literature. Oh, and pistachio ice-cream.

Both had been through a painful relationship. Beyond confessing the previous evening that they had been in love not too long ago, neither discussed the details of those past loves. Nevertheless, they could sense the depth of the anguish each other had suffered. Victoria knew when she met Bryan that her grieving period was coming to an end. Perhaps Bryan was experiencing the same metamorphosis. Maybe they were meant to meet each other just as a test. Just so that they could feel like there is life beyond their injured hearts; so that they could heal and then move on. They were distracters for each other.

Victoria wondered if it was possible to love someone so profoundly, lost him, and then to be able to replace that person with someone else. Not that Bryan was the someone else; it could be anyone. But could true love happen twice? Maybe the axiom that proclaims there is only one true love for every person is an aphorism that some morose philosophers invented in their brooding moments of darkness following some torturous love affair. Who made them the experts on love anyway? Why couldn't they write about recuperating, mending, and evolving? Or maybe that was the job of the psychoanalyst, not the poet or the philosopher.

"*Home sweet home!*" Victoria said to herself as the shuttle pulled up in front of her house.

No one was home, but the porch light was on. Victoria let herself in and closed the door behind her. She turned on a light and went into the living room. She sat on the sofa for a long time looking at the family portrait on the wall. It didn't include Tom; just the kids. Would Bryan look too young next to her in a family portrait? She shook her head as if to get thoughts of Bryan out of her mind.

Just then the phone rang and startled her. She ran into the kitchen and answered.

"I just wanted to make sure you got home safely," said Bryan on the other end of the line.

"I did!"

"Hey ..." he started.

"What?"

"Nothing." He paused for a moment. "Sweet dreams, Victoria."

*Maybe he does want to hang on my wall,* she thought to herself in amusement.

# CHAPTER TWENTY-SIX

The next morning Jennifer ran into her mother's bedroom and jumped on her bed.

"What did you bring back for me, mommy?!" she teased and kissed her mom on the cheek.

"Well, as a matter of fact, I did bring something back for you!" she answered.

"Mom, I was just kidding!"

"Go get the white box over on my dresser, sweetie."

Jennifer brought the box over to the bed and gingerly opened it.

"Oh, these earrings are beautiful, mom!" she exclaimed.

"A little old lady who lives in the mountains hand crafted them. She makes all kinds of necklaces and earrings, just like those, from clay that she gets somewhere in Yabucoa near her cabin. No one has been able to imitate the process she uses. They're not sure if the secret is in the clay, or the paints, or the glaze. Anyway, she's going to be one of our local artisans at the race site in December. We figure a lot of people will be doing last minute Christmas or Hanukkah shopping, so this will give the spectators something to do while they wait for their spouses or friends to run the marathon."

"What a great idea!" agreed Jennifer.

"So tell me, how did everything go here while I was gone?"

"Oh, we had some great wild parties! We only broke a few things," she teased, "and the dent in the car can be repaired in one day."

The phone rang downstairs and Jennifer ran down to answer it.

"It's for me, mom!"

Actually, Jennifer and Christopher had done a good job running the household for the week their mother was away. Chris was already living in his own apartment, but he had stayed with his sister at the house the week that Victoria was gone.

Jennifer was working as a camp counselor for the summer, and she loved it. She was very good with kids, and Victoria wondered if her daughter was going to follow in her footsteps and become a teacher, or maybe the marine biologist she had talked about in her junior year of high school. She did have a penchant for the outdoors. Victoria remembered when her daughter, at the age of four, would collect bugs and bring them back to the house in her plastic bug box. One day she caught a bee with her bare hands and put it in the box. When she was two, she collected a bunch of ants and put them in her pockets. On another occasion, she caught a grasshopper and took it to school for show and tell. By the fourth grade she had read every book on animals that she could get her hands on. She was always covered in dirt, and she could name just about any tree in the woods behind their house.

Christopher, on the other hand, had always been very pragmatic. He enjoyed nature, but he enjoyed numbers and logic even more. He was the kindest person. He wrote beautiful letters to his mom on Mother's Day and on her birthday, and he never forgot to call every week while in college. He was shy about asking for spending money in high school, and preferred to work and make his own way. Very independent.

Christopher was off to a good start in his career. Since he had gone to college with a full academic scholarship, his savings from high school and the planned pre-paid tuition money had never been touched. He had worked in the summers throughout his college years, and he had invested his earnings wisely with the guidance from his father. He had the backing of several investors for his business, and he was ready to open his own sportswear company. He was planning the grand opening for November. He had already worked through the details with the bank, a lawyer, and the family's accountant. Victoria thought that he was awfully young to be opening his own business; so inexperienced. There were so many athletic supply stores everywhere, so what would set this one apart from the others? Had he chosen the right location for his business? Would any of his trusted employees turn out to be thieves, as often was the case in retail? How would such a young entrepreneur handle that? Would distributors take advantage? But Victoria knew that Chris would be fine. Tom was helping him through many of the hurdles, and she knew he was very meticulous and savvy. She would just have to stop worrying...

"Mom," interrupted Jennifer, "while I was on the phone, someone else called. I clicked to the other line to see who it was, and it was someone named Bryan for you. He said he would call later."

"Oh, yes," Victoria offered quickly, "Bryan is my assistant race director." She would have to tell the kids about Bryan if he continued to call the house. No hiding this time. No secrets.

Bryan, Dan, Tom. They were so different, all of them. The only thing they had in common was their height; tall. *Very* tall. And their work ethic. All hard workers and passionate about what they did. But in retrospect, one thing that bothered Victoria about Tom was that he was perpetually late. He was late to dinner parties, kids' games, and the theater, to everything except work. Sometimes Victoria felt as if she had taken a back seat to his job. And then Dan had always been on time to everything. However, their contact had been so limited and controlled by time constraints, that maybe he wouldn't have been so punctual if they had had a normal relationship. And Bryan. In the little time they had spent together, he had been sometimes on time, and sometimes late. When he was late, he'd run up to spinning a tale about being stuck behind a herd of slow elephants, or some such thing. She smiled to herself at this thought.

Bryan was a breath of fresh air, though. He seemed to enjoy the simple pleasures of life, and their moments together had been uncomplicated. He was unpredictable to say the least. And fun.

All three men were also different with their displays of affection. Dan had been a very private person, and did not feel comfortable displaying affection in public, but he was very loving behind closed doors. He was caring. He had called her every morning to check in and ask about the details of her life. He was a good listener. He taught her many practical things, such as changing a tire on her car, upgrading the memory on her computer, how to shop for the best cell phone. He made her more aware of how to take care of her body, what to eat, and even how to dress more attractively. But Victoria was never quite sure if that wasn't for him as much as he said it was for her. He frowned when he didn't like something she wore or if she had gained any weight. She couldn't even eat cookies in front of him, or he'd take them away and ask her what she thought she was doing. Victoria wondered if Dan was doing the same to this new lady in his life or if it had only been with her. And she couldn't help wondering if he was as wonderful with this other lady in the bedroom as he had been with her. She felt tears well up in her eyes.

Tom, like Dan, had not been very affectionate in public. Not that Victoria had wanted this either, because she was a bit of a private person herself. But the difference was that he wasn't very affectionate at home, either. They had never talked about intimacy. They had just had sex every now and then when they thought enough time had passed. She knew in her heart that he had loved her, but the passion just wasn't ever there, not even in the first few years of the marriage.

Bryan had been loving and romantic and yet silly and playful. What a difference the age gap made! Or perhaps it wasn't really the age difference at all. Victoria didn't know why she couldn't just give him the credit for being as superb as he was. Maybe she was holding back, as she always did. Bracing herself for the fall. Maybe Bryan would just be her December romance, and after the race, he would be gone, and she could go back to her safe existence as Victoria Taylor, professor of English at Johns Hopkins University, and mother of two.

# CHAPTER TWENTY-SEVEN

"Mom, want to go for a little run?" Jennifer asked one day bouncing into her mother's room. "I have to stick to this summer training schedule my coach sent me from UVA."

"Sure!" responded Victoria. "Let me get changed real quick and I'll meet you on the porch!"

They drove to Columbia Park. No more street runs. Too dangerous. But then, parks aren't always as safe as they sound either. Two weeks earlier a female jogger had been bludgeoned with a hammer by some nineteen-year-old in a park nearby in pure daylight! The jogger had managed to escape and got to a road to hail down a car before passing out. The boy was arrested, so the story had a happy ending. But why are there so many nuts out there, thought Victoria, and what could they possibly have against runners?

"So this little kid at camp couldn't cross the stream and..."

"Jen," interrupted her mother as they ran across the bridge. "Do you think I could run a marathon again? Honest opinion!"

"Well, yeah, if you want to spend the rest of your life in a wheelchair!"

Victoria didn't react. She was lost in her thoughts.

"Mom, you're serious, aren't you?"

"Yes," answered Victoria in a whisper.

Jennifer stopped and stood in the path glaring at her mother.

"Come on, Jen," Victoria urged and motioned with her hand for her daughter to continue running. "You know, when I began running many years ago, the runner's behavior was considered errant; perhaps because they ignored the social pressures of their mundane existence, or because they became alienated from the mainstream. They probably seemed too elitist or stuck-up. Who knows? But women especially were criticized."

They ran past a pavilion where children were playing.

"But somewhere along the line," Victoria continued, "this behavior perceived as deviant became fashionable. It was further validated when researchers began studying the benefits of running to lessen the risk of heart disease."

"Mom, where are you going with this? You are like all over the place with this conversation, and you're not answering the question I asked. Why?"

"Okay, okay. I *am* going somewhere with this; just give me a moment. Anyway, all of a sudden, I was *allowed* to run. I was *commended* for running. Although your father never was too happy about it," she commented under her breath smiling. "But running became me. I became running. Intertwined somehow. When I was told to stop running after the accident, it was as if someone was telling me to stop being me. Stop existing. Am I making any sense now?"

"I guess," Jennifer responded with hesitation. "I understand how you feel, mom, and I know you want to run just one more marathon to prove whatever it is you have to prove. I know you are capable. But I just think that you'd be setting yourself up for a lot of unnecessary pain. Twenty-six miles is awfully far for someone your age with a bum hip."

Victoria laughed. "Getting *old*, am I?!"

"Mom! You know what I mean!"

"So what do you think about a half-marathon?"

"Well, that would be safer. I know you can cover the distance, mom. But you're not going to compete for time, are you?"

"No, no, no." Victoria hadn't really come to terms with that part.

"What race are you talking about, anyway?" asked her daughter.

"Puerto Rico in December."

They ran for awhile without talking. Finally Jennifer said "Well, you know your body. Please just don't compete for time, mom."

"Okay, you can even help me train just so you can keep me honest!"

"Deal. We can run on my slow days until I go to college next month. But no more than fifteen miles total, okay? Or I'll tell on you!"

# CHAPTER TWENTY-EIGHT

"Hello, Vicky?" asked Gabrielle on the other line. *"C'est moi!"*

"Gabi! It's been so long! Since May!"

"Only five months, *chère!"* Her French accent was stronger than ever!

"How is my sweet Jennifer doing at UVA?" she asked.

"Oh, Gabi, I miss her so much! It's a bit lonely without her smiley face around here! But she's doing well. And Christopher is doing well too."

"His business venture is good?"

"He's opening the shop formally next month in November, but he already has orders from some of the local high school for sports clothes and uniforms. Oh! And he has a girlfriend! I don't know how he has time for one, but he does!"

"She is nice?"

"Yes, very nice. And very patient. Mayia is a personal trainer, so they have a lot in common."

"A personal trainer? What is that?" Gabrielle asked.

"You know, like at an athletic club or spa. She sets up programs for people and works with them on reducing fat and toning up. I went to one of her aerobics classes, and boy did she make me feel old! I was hobbling out of there at the end, and she wasn't even breathing hard!"

"As much as you used to run? I'm sure you were in plenty good shape to keep up with her!" Gabrielle teased.

Victoria was tempted to tell her friend that she was still running, and that she was training for the half-marathon. But this wasn't the right time. She was afraid someone would try to stop her, and that someone would probably be her best friend Gabi. Too soon yet. Not even Bryan knew, even though she had alluded to it.

"And Jennifer is running okay on her team?" Gabrielle asked.

"It's going well. She's just a freshman on the team, so she's kind of average compared to the more seasoned runners. But the coach is impressed with her endurance and determination. She has grown taller these past couple of years, too, so the coach has her working on a different style of running than she had been accustomed to as a shorter person."

"Good! So she's having fun!"

"Yep! I'm going to go to one of her meets next weekend. I just wish it were closer to here. I do miss her."

"So if you get lonely, why don't you come and visit me in France and bring your Bryan with you?"

"Gabi, it's not like that with Bryan. He's just a good friend, okay?"

"Yes, yes, of course. So bring your good friend with you when you visit!"

"Anyway," Victoria tried changing the subject, "I can't go to France right now. I'm due back in Puerto Rico, and I'm right in the middle of my research project for the university."

"*Alors,* how is everything going for the big race?"

"Great! We're getting a very good response already! It is definitely a learning experience being on the other side as the organizer instead of a runner."

"Vicky, what shall I wear to Puerto Rico in December?"

"You're really going to go?"

"I would not miss it for *anything!*"

# CHAPTER TWENTY-NINE

The leaves were beautiful in October, thought Victoria on the drive to UVA to see Jennifer. The colors and the smells of autumn had a calming effect on her. Bryan was going with her to UVA to see Jennifer, and she was a bit nervous about it. They had already met each other, since Bryan had been around some weekends in the summer while Jennifer was still there. But Victoria had carefully presented him as the assistant race director and nothing more. It was a repetition of the pattern she had established with Dan. She hadn't wanted to bring someone home who could possibly disappear five months later. And yet, it had already been five months since Victoria had met Bryan, and he had assured her that he was not leaving. She believed him, although there was still a crumb of hesitance.

"We're here," she heard Bryan say. "Where is Jennifer's dorm?"

"Oh! Go right," she pointed, "and head towards the stadium."

Bryan had been sensing Victoria's hesitation about their relationship lately. He promised her one evening that he was not going anywhere; that as long as she had wanted him around, he would be there. Victoria recalled that same promise from Dan as vividly as if it had been made that morning. It had been on an early afternoon in October, just like this one. The air had been crisp, and Victoria remembered feeling chilled. She and Dan had driven to a park in separate cars so that she could get in a run before seeing him. They were to meet down by the stream on the small wooden bridge. She had arrived first. A few minutes later, she had spotted him jogging down the path towards her with his hand behind his back. He had produced a hand full of miniature daisies that he had seen along the way. They had talked for hours that day about the relationship, promises, and the future, as he had held her in his arms to shield her against the cold. Dan had told her that she was his best friend, and that no matter what happened to them in the future, he would always consider her as his best friend. He had asked her to never throw him away. But it hadn't been *her* who threw him away, had it?

"Victoria, are you okay, honey? Nervous about talking to Jennifer about us?" Bryan asked.

"What? Oh, yes. I guess I am," she responded.

As it turned out, Jennifer had already figured it out, and she was ecstatic about her mom finding someone *fun*, as she called it, to keep her company. All that worry for nothing! This seemed so easy. Everyone else was just fine with her having a boyfriend. Is that what you call it at this age? A boyfriend?

# CHAPTER THIRTY

In the weeks that followed her visit to UVA with Bryan, Victoria continued to train for the marathon. She had met with her doctor and got his clearance. He cautioned her about not pushing for a fast race, and to stick to her plan for the half instead of the whole marathon. She finally told Bryan that she intended to run the race. He was not happy, but he supported her in her dream. He offered to help her with anything that he could. She would need to count on him for the race-day final details. Once the race was underway, there wasn't much a director needed to do anyway. Everything would have been delegated. A director would only need to be available for emergencies. Bryan could handle that.

In November Victoria and Bryan went to Puerto Rico to meet with the staff one more time. Everything was coming together nicely. No threat of hurricanes, no unforeseen disasters. Two of the race assistants had fallen in love and were going to get married on the race date. Wow, so soon! But those things could happen when you were young and in love! Another member had had some kind of temper tantrum and quit the team. Good riddance. She was replaced immediately without any problem. You had to have the team on board with your vision, and if they couldn't see it, then it was time for them to move on. The hotel was booked to capacity and some runners were being obnoxious about reservations. Mr. Hernández was the consummate professional manager. He was booking people at other hotels and even making arrangements for their transportation back and forth to the race at the Rio Mar. People were coming from as far away as Sweden. Even some Cuban runners got into the mix somehow.

"Okay, Isabel, the registration packets look great. We're just waiting on that nutrition bar that will go in each packet, right?"

asked Victoria.

"Yes, and safety pins for the bib numbers. We have to bring those in from the mainland. But I have a question. Do we put the T-shirts for the pre-registered people in their packets, or do we keep them in the boxes and give them the sizes they ask for at the packet pick-up?"

"Leave them in boxes," Victoria responded. "But just give them the size they recorded on the registration form. We ordered the sizes accordingly, so we don't want to end up with a shortage for those who sent their forms in before the deadline. Anyone registering on-site will get whatever is left over. And then the pre-registrants can exchange sizes after the race if they want."

"Sounds good," responded Isabel.

"So do you have the current list of registrants? I'm curious to see if any of my former high school friends from the island are running. I probably won't recognize one name on the list because it has been so long since I've lived here!"

"Sure! The files are over in the corner with all the packets. I'll make you a copy of the list when I go downstairs."

"Okay, thanks." She turned to the crowd, "Well, everyone, I think that this is a wrap!"

The race had truly brought together a nice group of people, she mused. And it had raised thousands of dollars for the foundation already. Victoria felt a sense of accomplishment, and she was grateful that she could give back to this island that had helped her so much in her childhood. She loved the people, too.

"Okay," she continued, "let's finish up and get ready for dinner. This will be our last evening together before the race next month! We are going to celebrate tonight the engagement of Michal and Steve; toast to the birth of Frank's daughter Vanessa; and wish good luck to two of our assistants who have decided to run the marathon themselves! And let us not forget to pray each night for NO RAIN!" The crowd laughed and clapped.

Their last dinner together as a committee was at eight in the evening. Well, it got closer to nine. Puerto Rican time. Everyone was in a good mood. Most of the work was done, and only the fine details needed some work.

Victoria and Bryan sat at the table reminiscing about their first meeting there together. The dinner was wonderful, as always. The room was full of Latino humor and laughter. Then there was dancing. Victoria knew the *merengue* well because her step-father Antonio had taught her as a young girl. It appeared that Bryan knew the dance as well, and she observed that he was very good at it!

"I love you," he said, as they held each other on the dance floor.

Hearing the words aloud scared her. She knew that she loved him too, on some level, but she wasn't sure how, and she had been guarded with her feelings. Now that it was out there, she would have to face it. She didn't know what to respond. Was he waiting for her to say it too? And if she did, was it set in stone then? Were they officially a couple? Did this mean a future? Was she even marriage material?

Suddenly she realized the music had stopped and Bryan was leading her back to the table. The moment had passed as she had been deep in thought, and she had never responded to his declaration of love. She felt guilty. But in truth, she had felt too scared to seal the relationship with such strong words of affection. She didn't want Bryan to think that she was taking advantage of him and just using this relationship for companionship, and yet she wasn't sure if she was ready to have him think that she was totally committed to a future, to marriage. Oh God, *marriage?* She did care for him, and there was no one else in the picture. Was she just afraid of giving up that independence? Was she hesitant because he was younger than she? Certainly five years wasn't much of a difference! Then what was it?

Marriage wasn't easy. It was constant work. So many books had been written about keeping the marriage alive. Did she want that all over again? Tom and Victoria had never really worked at it. They had just lived comfortably with what they had. And then she had just woken up one morning knowing that it wasn't right. There had been no highs or lows, just co-existing. Going to work, coming home, having dinner and playing with the kids, and then she'd do school work as he would retreat to the basement to continue working on his projects. Victoria knew Tom had been content with this. He was a good man, loyal, and a good provider. But she hadn't been content.

Why was she even thinking about all of this right now?! Bryan had just said that he loved her, and wasn't that what any woman really wanted? To love and be loved?

"What's wrong, Victoria?" Bryan asked as he sat beside her at their table.

"Oh, nothing, Bryan. I was just going over the final details of the race in my mind. Last minute jitters."

"Stop worrying!" he laughed. "It's all under control, honey, and it will go off without a hitch!"

"Victoria!" Isabel waved as she came over and handed her some papers. "I almost forgot. Here is the copy of the race registration as you had asked."

"Oh yes, I had forgotten too," Victoria answered.

Bryan patted Victoria's hand. "There's Mario. I'm going to talk to my brother for a sec and I'll be right back."

Victoria unfolded the pages Isabel had given to her moments earlier. It really would be nice if some of her former friends from school had signed up to support the race. She had gone to a couple of high school class reunions, but she had only kept in touch with a few friends each year at Christmas when they all exchanged cards and wrote about their families and work. Now she wished she had contacted Anita Hernández and Jane Rullán personally to invite them to the event. And Jane was even a runner!

She absentmindedly scanned the first page, no recognizable friends there, the second page, and one cousin's name surfaced.

Nothing on the third page, and then there it was: a name she had never expected to see in a million years. Dan Cole. She looked again. How many Dan Cole's were there in the world? Certainly this wasn't *the* Dan Cole? And if it was, *why was he running in her race?!*

Victoria felt faint. She had to know who this was.

"Isabel," she interrupted as Isabel was speaking to another committee member.

"Isabel, *dónde están las registraciones?*" she whispered. "Are the applications still upstairs in the conference room?"

"*Sí,*" she replied. "Next to the boxes of T-shirts. *Problemas?*"

"No, not at all! I just want to check on one of the registrants on this list. I think it's someone I knew a long time ago!"

Victoria hurried out to the hall and down the steps to the Conference Center. She found the boxes. Isabel had been very organized, and all the entries were alphabetized and coded by sex and age groups.

Cole, Daniel. Male. Forty-eight. Residence: Arizona.

# CHAPTER THIRTY-ONE

"Hello, Christopher?"

"Hi, mom! How was your trip to Puerto Rico? Everything ready for the race?"

"Yes, "she replied, "we're all set! And we've raised quite a bit of money already for the Cancer foundation!"

"Great! And how is *your* training going?" he asked.

"She told you! That little sister of yours told you that I'm going to run the marathon!"

"*Half-marathon,*" he corrected her.

"Yes, yes, the *half.* So what do you think?"

"I think this is your run, mom. *Victoria's run,* at last."

"Thanks for your support, honey."

"But mom, you have to quit if your hip is telling you, okay?"

"Promise. I have a question for you." She took a deep breath. "Did you know that Dan Cole is running in the marathon?"

After a long pause, he sighed and answered "Yes, I knew."

"Well how did you know? And why didn't you tell me?"

"Mom, I found out from Adam just last month when he called to tell me he'd be coming to Maryland to see his mom in December for his break from law school. He said his dad had been training like a maniac in Arizona. And I didn't tell you for many reasons."

"Try some."

"Mom, you're nervous enough about this race. I knew you didn't need the added strain of knowing he was going to run. I thought that maybe he wouldn't really show up, or that maybe you wouldn't see him there. I thought that if you knew, maybe you'd want to throw in the towel for your own run."

"Okay, thanks, Chris. I'm so sorry to have asked you this and

155

put you on the spot. Thanks for being honest."

"Mom, that's not the only reason." He hesitated. Best to be honest. "Dan is engaged. He got engaged shortly after we saw him at the graduation in May."

"Okay. Okay." She summoned courage, not really knowing how she felt about it. "Thanks for telling me, Chris. I know that was tough for you. But I'm okay, you know? Bryan is a big part of my life now. I just like knowing what is going on, you know?"

"I know, mom."

# CHAPTER THIRTY-TWO

"Home for the holidays!" blurted out Jennifer as she exploded through the front door and threw her suitcases to the side. "I just *love* Thanksgiving!" she exclaimed.

Victoria ran to the door to greet her daughter who was home from college for the holiday.

"Where's the turkey, mom?!"

"No turkey. We're having lasagna," she teased, as she continued making her pumpkin caramel pie.

"*MOM!*"

"Okay! It's out in the fridge in the garage."

"*That's* what I want to hear!" She came back into the kitchen two minutes later. "Big turkey, mom. How many people are we having?"

"Tons! So I'll need your help tomorrow, okay? Let's see, Aunt Rina and Rob, Grandma, Chris and Mayia…"

"Is Aunt Gabi coming?"

"No. She has a big dinner planned in Paris, even though they don't really celebrate Thanksgiving there. She just invites all her American friends. Don't ask me what she cooks, but it probably isn't a turkey! But she'll be coming to the race in December, sweetie, so we'll see her then. Oh, and Bryan and his mom are coming tomorrow, too."

"Chris told me that Adam is coming in to town to see his mom. Do you think we could invite him, or is it too last minute?"

"Chris already invited Adam and another friend. He said that Adam is eating at his mom's, but he'll come by for dessert later on."

Thanksgiving dinner was great. There was plenty of food, and they even had leftovers, since everyone had insisted on bringing a dish of something to add to the ton of food they already had. Most people brought desserts. No fruitcake allowed, though.

"Adam is here," Mayia said as she walked into the kitchen where Bryan and Victoria were washing dishes.

"Just in time for dessert," Victoria said. "Mayia, can you please check to see how many people want coffee?"

"Sure!"

Mayia was going to make a perfect wife for Christopher someday. Victoria figured they were headed in that direction. She was glad they were going to wait a bit to get married, though. They were a lot alike and had similar interests. They had opened the business two weeks before Thanksgiving, and they had survived the opening without killing each other! Mayia had worked in the summers as an athletic trainer while going to college, so she had plenty of experience to bring to the business. Her degree had been in sports medicine. She knew sports in general and running in particular. She knew shoes, too. She had even convinced Victoria that she had been wearing the wrong type of running shoe. Victoria had always worn the same type of shoe, same company. But the company she liked kept changing the design of its shoes, for whatever reason. They had put some type of bubble in the heel, and it was obnoxious. It kept squeaking. And they were changing the shape of the toe box. Not good. So Mayia examined Victoria's worn-out shoes and recommended a new kind with more cushioning in the heel, a looser toe box, and a better arch. Victoria was impressed.

Mayia was going to join Christopher in Puerto Rico for the two-day Health and Fitness Expo prior to the race. Victoria's committee had invited some top health and fitness experts, and there would be plenty of vendors there as well. Christopher would be talking about athletic apparel that would enhance performance. Jennifer had told him about a four-year study that was conducted at the UVA Center for Sports Medicine that showed how the type of athletic apparel worn during exercise showed significant improvements in force and power production. Chris researched the study and brought that expertise to his clothing line for marketing purposes. Mayia was going to be talking to the crowds about losing body fat versus weight for increased performance. She'd show that weight is not an indicator of fitness and she would talk about a fitness program and diet. Then she would demonstrate some of the items they were selling that could help, such as the body fat monitor scales; biomechanical hands grips used during runs to improve equilibrium and form; a new sports drink powder that releases energy for hours; and a heart rate monitor for entry level runners and another for serious runners.

"Hi, guys!" Adam said as he entered the kitchen and gave everyone a hug. "Mom sent this dessert. Where should I put it?"

*More dessert*, thought Victoria. "On the table in the dining room, Adam. That was very thoughtful of her! I'm taking orders for coffee," said Victoria. "Do you want some?"

"Yes, please. I'm going to go find Chris. I heard his first two weeks at the store went well!"

"Yes, they did! He's downstairs with the others assembling the electric train for Christmas. I know, I know! This family has a thing about Christmas! I'm going to bet we'll even be watching the Christmas videos before the night is over!"

Victoria and Bryan were quiet for a few moments as he continued drying the dishes and she looked for cups for the coffee.

"So that was Dan's son," he finally said.

"Yes," she answered.

After finding out that Dan was going to run in the marathon, Victoria had felt compelled for some reason to just tell Bryan all about the past relationship. Well, most of it, anyway. She didn't tell him about the intense love that she and Dan had shared, the promises they had made, or the hours of fulfillment she had cherished. She told Bryan that Dan had been one of her coaches and that they had had an affair. Even thought they had both been separated from their spouses at the time, she had still considered it an affair, because they had kept it so secret from everyone. She wasn't sure why she had felt the need to share all of this with Bryan, but she had wanted him to know that she wasn't perfect, and that she had been vulnerable and she had allowed for Dan to have an inexplicable control over her. She wanted to make sure that the remnants of that relationship were not influencing the present relationship. She told him that she always felt like she had on her guard, but that she didn't want to feel that way with him.

Bryan had responded only as Bryan would, being the wonderful person that he was. He had told her that maybe Dan had been sent to her as a distracter while she had been going through a tough divorce, and that maybe she and Dan had not really been meant to be together for the long term. Maybe her feelings for Dan had been intensified as she had desperately sought to define love after losing her marriage.

How could Victoria explain to Bryan that Dan had been so much more than a distracter? There wasn't anything she wouldn't have done for Dan had he asked her. She had fallen for him with all her soul. She had thought about him every day and had felt his presence in everything she did. He wasn't a distracter. He couldn't have been a crush or an infatuation. She had dreamed of becoming a blended family with him and their three children. She had pictured their life and jobs and retirement, the white picket fence and the two dogs. Popcorn and movies, walking in the parks, and home-cooked dinners. They had been together for almost two years, and then she had walked in and seen him in the arms of another woman. That had been the end of a two-year dream and the rest of her confidence in men.

But Victoria had felt good about telling Bryan the story; about being truthful. She felt closer to him. She didn't want any secrets. Dan probably would have said that she didn't tell Bryan the whole story, because she didn't even know the story. How could she have known who the other woman was and how insignificant she had been in Dan's life?

What Victoria didn't know was that the brunette had been working in Dan's architectural firm for a while. Dan didn't know how long, because he hadn't really noticed her. She was his partner's secretary, and when the two partners had started working on a project together, she became part of the mix. It had started innocently enough with the brunette talking about her fiancée, but at one point he realized that she had wanted more. One night as they worked late at the office, she had kissed him. He had felt guilty, but he had wanted more. He would never hurt Victoria intentionally; he loved her. He had explained this to the brunette. But it was hard to get the kiss out of his mind, so he began justifying his motives as he considered the strained relationship with Victoria. And yet, his relationship with Victoria had felt clandestine only because he had wanted it that way. He had told her that they were both going through final stages of divorce, and that he wasn't ready for the children or his friends or family to know that he had jumped into another relationship so quickly. He didn't want the gossip or the advice about rebound relationships. Victoria had respected his wishes to keep the relationship secret. But Dan's plan had backfired in a sense, because he grew tired of meeting her in secluded places, only on days when their former spouses had the children, and only for short amounts of time. He was tired of pining away the hours at his office late at night just waiting for Victoria to call. He was lonely. It was at this low point that he had allowed the brunette into his life. They carried on with a physical relationship, although never consummating it, in the sense of the word, but enjoying every other physical pleasure. Dan had been filled with guilt and anxiety the whole time that he had been carrying on with the secretary. He began taking it out on Victoria and started picking on her for insignificant things. They fought constantly, and Dan was defensive about everything. Victoria was confused. She had understood only that she was causing Dan an increased amount of stress, and that perhaps he had been feeling regret about their relationship. He continued punishing Victoria with his confusing messages, or at least that's what it had felt like at the time. He had cut her off when she started talking about the future, and he had started to tell her that he was not worthy of her. She still had not been able to understand what was going on.

Dan had asked himself repeatedly what he was doing. He loved Victoria. The brunette was a nameless person who had passed him on the road to his future. Now he was hurting two women, because the secretary was totally dedicated to him. She secretly called him, sent him letters, cooked for him, and brought him little presents. Victoria figured out later that she had probably been the reason as to why Dan didn't want Victoria to be in his apartment while he was not there. He was probably afraid that the secretary would call and leave one of her messages and that Victoria would hear it. Or that maybe the brunette would just drop in on a surprise visit only to find Victoria there. He was a mess. He had wanted to get out of the whole thing. He had called the secretary to come into his office that day to let her know that he had made a mistake, and that he couldn't continue the relationship. She had a fiancée, after all. She deserved the fiancée, because he was a good person, and they were surely meant for each other. The brunette had cried and begged, and it was at that point that Victoria had walked into Dan's office so long ago to find the brunette in his arms.

Victoria had run out to her car that day after seeing them together, and she had driven away as quickly as she could. She had not wanted to hear Dan's explanation, because it was all clear to her, and there was no excuse that could ever fix what she had just witnessed. All the details had started coming to her in flashes: why he had been picking fights, why he had not wanted her to come to his apartment anymore, why he had asked her to leave one time saying that his ex-wife was coming over to deliver some of Adam's clothes. She had remembered one time when Dan said he would have to go out on a date with someone somewhere along the line so as to deflect attention from his friends who were always trying to set him up with blind dates. So why hadn't he just told his friends about her? Surely this other person had been the reason as to why he had not wanted her to bring their relationship out into the open.

Victoria had been angry, hurt, confused and embarrassed. She had felt guilty. But why? She had felt as if she had been keeping Dan from living his life, from healing from his divorce. She remembered how sometimes she'd be so confused over things he'd say on the phone, details would get turned around, he'd become nasty for no apparent reason, and she would end up hanging up the phone. She would later call back to apologize, and he's say to her "it's that simple, isn't it? That simple to just walk away from me?" She would be devastated that he hadn't understood at all. She had been losing control of who she was. She hadn't even been sure if her thoughts were her own. It had been at this point that she should probably have left the relationship. But she had tried to leave, hadn't she? When she had talked to him about her doubts, he had cried and made her feel guilty about not sticking to her promise to be with him forever. On the day that she had walked into his office and found him with the secretary, it had not been simple at all. It had been final. She was not going to stand in his way any longer.

Victoria remembered driving through the rain that afternoon when she had left Dan's office. She had been wracked by pain and had been crying so hard that she had had to pull over to the shoulder of the road at one point. Then she had let the car steer her to the park where she and Dan had met on occasion to run and talk about life and their dreams. The rain had stopped. She had walked to the bridge they had traversed on so many of those runs. This was where he had given her the gold bracelet as a promise of his

163

love and commitment earlier in the relationship. After that, she had gone to the bridge whenever she had wanted a few moments alone just to think, because she had felt secure there. On this day, however, she had felt quite the opposite. There had been no solace for her. She had let out loud sobs as she held her arms across her chest and rocked back and forth. She couldn't figure out if this had all been his fault or her fault; that maybe she had pushed him too hard, demanded too much of their relationship. She couldn't bear the thought of him in bed with someone else. It had been too much for her to handle, and she thought that she would never get through the ordeal. But she had been a survivor when her sister had died, and then her step-father, and she had moved to Europe and regained control of her life, hadn't she? Hadn't she had the courage to divorce Tom when their life had been at a stalemate? Hadn't she made it through the pain of her surgery after the accident, and missing the Olympics? Surely this was not as hard as any of those times. She could get through this.

It had been getting late that day in the park and the sun was setting. It was time to go; time to get back to her life. She stood up from where she had been sitting on the bridge, took off the bracelet that Dan had given her, and she left it on the side of the bridge. "This is meant for someone else," she had said.

Dan had driven around in the rain looking for Victoria that evening. Her car had not been at home. It had not been at the grocery store where she usually went on Tuesday nights after work. He had driven around the university. No Victoria. She would not answer her cell phone. He had waited outside her home. Finally at dusk he went to the park to see if she had been there, but there had been no sign of her. He got out of his car and walked to the bridge where he had remembered bringing her daisies so long ago at the beginning of their relationship. He had stood there and cried. He knew that it was over. *What had he done?* He couldn't have even defended himself if he had had the opportunity to talk to her. And even if he had, what would he have said? Would it have changed her mind to know that it was all clear to him now, that he didn't want the brunette, and that he was ready to profess his love to her and yell it out to anyone who would listen? He would try. He had dried his tears and determined that he would try. He would make it up to her. But he knew that things would not be able to go back to normal. When faced with tragedy, one never went back to normal; rather a new sense of normalcy was created with whatever variables were remaining. Surely they could do that.

Victoria, meanwhile, had gone to a bagel shop near her home after the time she had spent at the park. She had just needed a little more time to think before going into the house and facing the details of her life. She had been summoning her strength and resolve. She would not look back. She would not blame herself or Dan for the past two years. It was time to get back to her wonderful children, her career, and her friends. She drove to her house and went inside.

Victoria had never seen Dan's car parked at the corner. As Dan saw her walk into the house and close the door behind her, he sighed with relief just knowing that she had come home safe. He scrounged around on the floor of his car amongst papers and maps and found an empty envelope. He wrote on the front of it "To Victoria." He pulled out of his pocket the gold bracelet that he had found on the bridge and dropped it into the envelope. He got out of his car and walked up to her mailbox. He had stood there for a long moment hoping for a miracle, that perhaps she would see him and come outside. There was none. He left the envelope in her mailbox, got into his car, and drove away from the one woman who he had ever loved.

# CHAPTER THIRTY-THREE

The week after Thanksgiving, Victoria began making plans with Christopher and Jennifer to meet in Puerto Rico for the race. They would be meeting her on the morning of the 10th and the race was scheduled for Sunday the 12th. Victoria was going to be flying down ahead of them. She discussed flight information and the plans to pick them up at the airport. Jennifer would still be in college at that time, but she had taken off that Friday so she could fly to Puerto Rico from Virginia. She was so grown up and independent!

Victoria had not known that back in Arizona, Dan was also telling his son Adam about his plans to fly to Puerto Rico for the race. His company had always made some big donations at the end of the tax year to various charities in South America. Dan had convinced them to sponsor him for the race, so he would be representing the company with their donation this year. Adam had asked if Anne, Dan's fiancée, would be going with him to the race.

"No," Dan had told his son. "Anne is going to be in Tucson on a strict schedule to finish remodeling a home for some tycoon that bought an old orphanage and is converting it into a house. She has six weeks to do the job, so she is racing against the clock!"

If truth be known, Dan had discouraged Anne from coming on the trip. She had said that she could get away for a weekend and join him if he had wanted, but he told her that he was just fulfilling an obligation for work and would not be there long enough for them to have fun.

Dan had decided to run the marathon because it was the only way he had thought that he could make a connection with Victoria. He had to know if she had found happiness. Surely she had. Dan had continued on with his life when he moved out to Arizona, but in the back of his heart, he wished he had tried harder to make contact with Victoria prior to leaving. There hadn't been any closure to what had happened. He had just wanted to explain it all; to say sorry.

Dan was happy enough with Anne, he reflected. He had met her at his architectural firm in Arizona when the company had decided that they needed a new image. They had hired Anne to do the remodeling. She had told the president of the company that his lobby was a mish-mash of overstuffed chairs and ugly wooden sculptures thrown together in an attempt to say something. "They say nothing," she had said. Dan was smitten when he heard this brash commentary. He found Anne to be a bit eccentric and outspoken, but he had also found her to be smart and to have a good sense of humor. She was tall with dark brown hair cut in a page-boy look, and she had greenish-yellowish eyes. She dressed a bit flamboyant for his gusto, but his interest had definitely been piqued. They had been together since that day.

Dan remembered taking Anne to the cousins' graduation at James Madison in May. She had wanted to go east to see the capital city. Why not? Why should he hide her from Victoria? After all, Victoria had thrown him away without allowing him to explain the secretary, so she certainly wouldn't care who he was with at this point. But he still couldn't help but wonder. He had just wanted a brief moment with Victoria at the graduation; just time enough to explain and to see how she was doing. Maybe a moment to ask forgiveness. He would be able to stop feeling so awful about the whole episode and would be able to move on. But the timing had all been wrong. There had been no moment for the explanation or for forgiveness.

# CHAPTER THIRTY-FOUR

"Bryan, do you have the laptop?" asked Victoria nervously as they sat at Baltimore International Airport waiting for their flight to be called. He nodded. "And what about the tickets?"

"Calm down, sweetie," he replied, "I have the laptop, tickets, toothpaste, you name it! And if we forgot something, we'll buy it in Puerto Rico!"

They finally heard their flight being called to board for Puerto Rico.

It was Monday. Six more days until the race. Victoria was a little more nervous than she had anticipated. The details of the race didn't bother her as much as the run itself. Had she prepared enough for this run? Her longest run had been nineteen miles. In the back of her mind she still toyed dangerously with finishing the whole marathon. But seventeen miles was hardly enough training to perform a full 26-mile marathon. Too late now. This week she would have to taper her running; that was the rule. She would run three miles today, five on Tuesday, four on Wednesday, about three on Saturday, and then the marathon. The *half-marathon,* she reminded herself.

They got to their seats and Victoria rested her head on Bryan's shoulder trying not to think about the race. She stared out of the window next to Bryan and listened to the voices of the flight attendants and the passengers around them.

"Are you nervous?" Victoria heard a man ask someone behind them.

"Not too much. I trust the pilot," the young woman sitting next to him replied. The couple was sitting a few rows back and to the left of them.

"Not about the flight, honey, I mean about the race."

"A little!" the lady responded. "I can't believe we are actually going to do a marathon on our honeymoon! You know that our friends think we are crazy, right?" she laughed.

"I know! But we really lucked out with our timing. And we were so lucky to get a reservation for the Rio Mar hotel. All the hotels in the area were packed!"

"I think it's because a lot of runners are coming to support this Victoria lady since she had been such a good runner herself and a big spokesperson for women in racing. I read about her in my runner's magazine."

"What was her story again?" the husband asked.

"She started running in Puerto Rico when she was young, and she kind of paved the way for women in the event, especially Latino women."

"So I guess she's older and can't run, so they asked her to be the sponsor of the race?"

"Women are never too old to run!" the new bride retorted. "I just want to meet her, you know? I read that her little sister died, and they think that's why she started running. Kind of like my story." The bride looked out the window into the clouds as her new husband put his hand on hers.

"I tried getting the tickets to the pre-race dinner so you could meet her, but they were sold out. I promise that I will figure out a way for you to meet her, though, okay?"

His wife smiled.

The groom felt someone tap him on the shoulder and he saw a woman in the aisle standing next to him.

"These are for you," she said, holding out two tickets to the man and his wife.

"What?" he asked the stranger a bit confused.

"Two complimentary tickets to the head table." She pushed the tickets into his hand. "For the pre-race dinner on Saturday."

"Wow! Thanks! Why are *we* getting these?!"

"You're newlyweds, right?" she asked. "Well, Puerto Rico

takes good care of honeymooners!"

He stared down at the tickets in his hand. "How did *you* get these?"

"I have connections," replied Victoria with a smile as she turned and walked back to her seat.

"Wow!" he said again to his new wife. "How did that lady know we needed tickets? And who the heck was she, anyway?"

"Victoria," his wife responded with a smile. "That was Victoria."

"We're here!" exclaimed Bryan to Victoria who was sleeping on his shoulder in the seat next to him. "*La Isla del Encanto!*"

They arrived at the hotel and were promptly met by Mr. Hernández and Ms. Santos in the lobby to help them with whatever needed to get done prior to the event on the weekend. They informed Victoria that members of the race committee had been arriving all day from the mainland and other parts of the island. All of the committee members would probably be there by Wednesday, and most of the runners would arrive on Friday and Saturday.

Mr. Hernández assured them that the Conference Center was ready for the seminars and the expo on Friday. Ms. Santos talked to Victoria about the tours and activities planned for the pre and post race crowd. The racers wouldn't be drinking, but their families and the volunteers would, so the thatched huts on the beach were stocked and ready to go. All kinds of carb-loading foods and pasta were being prepared for the pre-race dinner on Saturday. A local artist was busily working on an ice carving of a runner with wings for show at the dinner. The *Ballet Folklórico* would arrive on Friday and would perform on Saturday after the dinner. The local artisans and crafters would be setting up their booths outside the lobby near the pool in the next couple of days.

The hotel was decorated with hundreds of red Poinsettias

since it was so close to Christmas. There were white twinkling lights all along the pool area outside and on every bridge that traversed the pool. Lanterns with bright red bows hung from the palm trees outside. Gold balls and green garland twisted around the brass railings of the staircases. There was a tall pine tree in the center of the lobby that was decorated with locally crafted ornaments in all sizes and shapes.

A chocolatier had created pairs of miniature chocolate jogging shoes to put on the pillow of each guest as a courtesy. It had been either the chocolate shoes or a nutrition gel. Victoria chose the chocolate, of course. There were small baskets of fruit in each room, a container of a leading sports drink on the counter, and fresh white towels with blister kits in the bathrooms. "Blister kits?" Victoria had asked one of the committee members. "New promotion from some company" had been the response. *Nice touch*, thought Victoria.

This was going to be a spectacular event, and Victoria was so excited. She wanted to show off her little island and she was so proud of all the people that had put in so much effort into making this race and the Cancer fundraiser such a success. It wasn't just for charity. This event would show outsiders how truly beautiful Puerto Rico is and how kind the people are. The island was bathed in Christmas lights from the lonely streets of the *caseríos* near the airport to the busy cobblestone streets of Old San Juan. The weather was ideal---84 degrees. The water was calm and translucent, and the white sand blended with mica to sparkle in the sun.

There were musicians in the lobby in their white *guayaveras* and they were receiving instructions from Ms. Santos for the upcoming events. Everything appeared to be in order. "*Fiesta!*" she whispered to herself.

# CHAPTER THIRTY-FIVE

*"Oye, Ramón, qué es el amor para tí?"* Victoria asked her buddy at the hut on the beach. She was waiting for Bryan. They were going to go to Old San Juan for one last dinner alone before all the people began arriving and vying for their time and attention. *"What is love?"* Ramón thought aloud. "You ask a very difficult question, *Señora.*" He continued wiping down the bar and washing glasses. There wasn't anyone else around, so Victoria took the opportunity to engage him in conversation.

"Okay, so why do you love your wife?" she persisted.

"She is a wonderful woman," he began with his heavy accent. "I could not choose a better mother for my children. She makes all their meals, she washes their clothes and dresses them nicely every day; she drives them to school and soccer; she talks to their teachers; and she helps them with homework. She takes good care of me and never complains. She is a very positive person." He looked at her inquisitively. "So, what can I get for you to drink, *Señora?*"

"I guess a Chardonnay," she replied.

Ramón was quick to assess her mood. "We have a very nice Viognier from Porter Creek Vineyards in the Russian River Valley. Mario went there this summer and bought all the cases they had. It's just a small winery, but with a big taste. We don't serve it to everybody," he smiled. "*Lo recomiendo.*"

"Sure, I'll try it," she smiled back.

But Victoria wasn't too interested in the wine, rather in what Ramón had just said about love. She thought that it was sad that people would confuse the love of a woman with the love of a mother. So many people seemed to do that; put their children first and the marriage second.

"*Salud,*" Ramón said bringing her the glass of wine and placing it in front of her on the bar.

"*Buenísimo!*" she offered her approval.

"Back to your question," he said. "Do you permit me to speak freely?"

"Yes, yes, please!"

"Okay. Happiness is the primary need of all of us; we don't like pain, no?"

"I follow," she said.

"So, there is a balance. We can derive happiness from what we achieve on our own, but sometimes sacrificing and making others feel happy makes us happy too. When you just rely on someone else to make you happy, it affects the relationship in a bad way. Bad attitude. So you make the other person happy and give him or her a chance to make you happy. Both need to show care for each other."

"But how do you know you are making that other person happy?" she asked.

"We do not let that fear overpower the relationship, *verdad*? You just give. Expect nothing. Be compassionate and be open. Do not hide anything."

That was it, thought Victoria. *Do not hide anything.* That was the key!

"Explain," she said.

"Believe. Trust. At the beginning when you first meet someone, you believe in him without knowing much about him or his character, yes? But as the relationship grows, there should be no doubt about that trust, so it is important to tell everything as soon as possible."

"For example?" she asked.

"For example, if you have a fear of rejection, you tell the other person. Do not let it overpower the relationship. Stop trying to be perfect, because it just causes stress. Tell the person about the concerns and the fear. You will be surprised what happens when you do not hide your feelings and your concerns."

Excellent. Ramón had just been vindicated. He must have figured Victoria was too smart to accept the *macho* speech about the wife being a good mother. His advice would be well taken. Victoria knew what she had to do. Tonight. Tonight she would tell Bryan all that was left in her heart about her past with Dan, her fear of trusting another man, and her fear of not deserving the love of another man. She would tell him about her preoccupation with needing to be perfect. Bryan was compassionate and would help her through this. She already felt her love for Bryan growing with this simple realization.

"So what do you think?" asked Ramón.

"I think you are a wise man and that your wife is very lucky," she replied.

"Thank you. But I meant about the wine. Good, no?"

Victoria blushed about the confusion.

"Absolutely!" she responded. "It's good enough to make your clothes fall off!"

They both laughed aloud.

"This Mr. Bryan is a lucky man too, *Señora*!"

# CHAPTER THIRTY-SIX

The old town of San Juan was tastefully decorated for the holidays. The streets were illuminated with soft white lights at every corner and on every tree. Wooden shutters opened onto the sidewalks and a soft glow emanated from behind lace curtains. Peoples' excited voices traveled through the wrought iron gates of the houses as they planned and prepared for the *posadas*. The smells that spilled out onto the streets were indescribable! Puerto Rican food was not spicy like Mexican food. But there was something there, in every dish, which tempted the most finicky of eaters. Victoria knew many of the secrets of the *sasón* used in these dishes, because her grandmother had taught her how to cook when she was in high school on the island.

Victoria and Bryan walked along the streets until they reached the intersection of Calle Cristo and Calle de San Sebastián. She pointed down the street to the Capilla de Cristo, a chapel at the *Parque de las Palomas*, or Pigeon's Park. She told Bryan about the time she had taken Christopher and Jennifer to the park to feed the pigeons, and Jennifer had the pigeons eating sunflower seeds out of her hands!

"Okay, now you have to see this," she pointed up the street in the other direction at the Cathedral of San Juan. "It's special to me."

Bryan and Victoria walked along the sidewalk the short distance to the cathedral.

"Does it look familiar?" she asked.

"Not really. Why?"

"Do you remember the small yellow ceramic cathedral that Jennifer made for me in her ceramics class last year that's in my bedroom at home? This was the model for the cathedral! See the three arches in the front?"

Victoria explained how she had taken an art classes with an instructor named Hector Mayol in this cathedral when she was a teenager living in Puerto Rico. The class had only had five people in it, but she had loved taking the bus to this church to paint and explore the world of canvas and oils.

"The cathedral had originally been built in 1540, but it was destroyed by a hurricane in 1584. So they rebuilt it in 1592 in the same style as they had done before the destruction. Sometime we'll take a closer look inside. They have a ton of relics from Ponce de León under preservation in the church. It's nice."

Then they walked across the street and entered El Convento, a 16th century former convent that had been turned into a series of restaurants and a small hotel. It was a gorgeous pale yellow and cream-colored building. The hotel had two floors of restaurants, cafés, art galleries and shops. They entered through the lobby and stopped in the interior courtyard to marvel at the 350-year-old tree. As they looked up to see the top of the tree, they saw mahogany beams on the ceilings surrounding the rest of the lobby, and beautiful romantic oil paintings and tapestries hanging on the walls. The lobby was filled with handcrafted furniture on Andalucian tiles for the floors.

They were escorted upstairs to the *Picoteo Restaurant and Bar*, a rooftop sundeck fringed by *bougainvillea* with views of Old San Juan. The sun was setting as they looked out onto the old cobblestone roads below.

The dinner was just as wonderful as had been recommended by Mr. Hernández back at the Rio Mar. The best part, however, had been the conversation. Victoria had in fact shared all of the thoughts she had had that afternoon when she had been waiting for Bryan at the bar and talking to Ramón. *Hide nothing*, he had said, and she did just that. She had told Bryan everything there was to tell.

"I have something to share as well," he said. "I wasn't sure if it was important, but I want you to also know my pain after sharing your own. I was engaged before I met you."

*Oh my God!*

"Well, about five years before meeting you," he corrected.

Victoria sighed heavily and listened intently. Ramón had said to share and to hide nothing, so this was Bryan's turn.

Bryan explained that he had dated a medical intern at Georgetown University Hospital. They had met at a party when they were in their early 30s. Since they were both workaholics, their friends had set them up for the occasion. He was mesmerized from the first day they had met. She was intelligent and very compassionate. They had a difficult courtship at the beginning because there wasn't ever much time to be together. Eventually he had asked her to move in with him so that they could spend some time together, and she had accepted. The relationship was one that existed only in fairytales, except for the time constraints. Bryan had dated other women before her and had had crushes before, but he was truly in love with Sarah. On the night that they were to get engaged, Bryan was left waiting at the restaurant with a yellow diamond ring in a small black velvet box. He had been devastated. He found out later that evening that Sarah had not left him intentionally. She had been hit by a car leaving work and had suffered irreparable brain damage. She was in a coma. He had been with her parents several months later when they made the difficult decision to take her off of the respirator, and she peacefully passed away the next day.

# CHAPTER THIRTY-SEVEN

Saturday morning arrived too quickly. Only one more day until the race, and the forgotten small details were surfacing at an alarming rate!

"Okay, Bryan. The committee will meet from 9:00 a.m. to noon today," she said while dressing. "And then don't forget the private luncheon with our corporate sponsors."

"Where is that again?" he yelled from the bathroom where he was showering.

"Agh! I forgot!" she answered. "But I'll ask Ms. Santos. Anyway, at two o'clock the seminars begin, and then cocktails at six, and the dinner at eight."

"Okay, in case I lose you in the havoc today, *I love you.*"

"I love you too," she said, and she meant it.

Bryan came out of the bathroom with a towel around his waist as Victoria was putting on her shoes. "Starting time tomorrow is at eight sharp, right?" he asked.

"Yes, but I'm going to need you out there at six in the morning."

"Ouch!" he said laughing. "I'm teasing! You know I'll be there, honey. Anything you say!"

"Are you sure you don't mind overseeing everything from start to finish while I'm running?" she asked with some hesitation.

"Victoria," he said taking her into his arms, "everything is in great shape. All the details will come together today, and tomorrow will be a day to celebrate!"

He kissed her on the head and then smoothed her hair down and looked at her face.

"I just hope," he said slowly, "I hope that you won't hurt yourself, Victoria."

"Bryan…"

"Shh," he cut her off. "I know. Victoria can take care of herself! I trust you."

The committee had everything in order, just as expected. The past two days had actually gone rather smoothly. Registration was complete and packets had been prepared with the running bibs and the micro-chips for shoes. All the electronic equipment was ready. The course had been measured long ago and had been painted. Police were ready. Ambulances ready. Timers, water stops, food, medals, trophies, prizes, all ready. The financial sponsors were awaiting endorsements, and the press was ready for the coverage.

Victoria breezed through the morning meetings, hosted the luncheon for the financers, and then stopped to check on the seminars and Expo. She walked through the back doors of the Conference Center and looked inside. She could see Christopher and Mayia next to their booth, and she saw that Jennifer was getting a kick out of promoting her brother's business as well! She walked over to one of the small rooms where they were hosting a seminar on pre and post race hydration and nutrition and walked to the back of the room and stood leaning on a window.

Dan Cole couldn't concentrate on the seminar. He was distracted. He kept wondering why he hadn't run into Victoria yet, at least to say hello.

He knew that he was only running this marathon in hopes of seeing her. But the training had not really been that bad, he thought. He had discovered some interesting paths through the mountains in Arizona when he ran his long runs on the weekends. The Catalinas, Mount Lemon, Apache Peak---all astonishingly beautiful. On one of his trips to the Oracle mountains, he and Adam had met a rancher who owned the High Jinks property. The old man had taught Dan about the cacti and flora, about stones, creeks, fires, animals and snakes. Dan enjoyed his visits to Apache Mountain where the rancher preserved and shared stories of Bill Cody's legacy as they sat around a fire with plenty of beer at hand. Running wasn't boring there.

Dan looked toward the window deep in thought and suddenly he saw her. *It was Victoria.*

He tried to politely get out of his aisle in the front of the room by stepping over pairs of long athletic legs and tripping over one little girls' doll buggy. By the time he turned and headed for the window on the far side of the room, she was gone. He rushed outside, but Victoria was nowhere.

Victoria hadn't seen him.

# CHAPTER THIRTY-EIGHT

Puerto Ricans customarily ate the evening meal late. No set time; just late. Dinner was always on the stove for whoever dropped in to eat. Usually there wasn't any warning; you just showed up. You didn't need to bring a bottle of wine or flowers or candy. Just come prepared to eat two plates of everything! Never talk about politics during the meal. Or money, or sex, or religion. Never. Puerto Ricans did not like to argue during the dinner. It was disrespectful to the hostess. Tempers could flare, and there was always the inevitability that someone would have to storm away from the table. And you *never* abandoned your food! So family and friends kept away from controversial topics of conversation until after the meal.

The dinner at the hotel this evening, however, was starting much earlier than by Puerto Rican standards. People would generally arrive on time to this dinner. There would be pasta instead of rice and beans, but there would be plenty of other delicacies for the families of the runners to enjoy. People would definitely be talking about politics, money and religion. And running.

The dining room had been decorated with pink Poinsettias and silver ornaments. Each table was covered with a white linen cloth accompanied by pink linen napkins. The silver and crystal were spotless, and the white china reflected the spray of miniature white lights hanging from palm trees that were strategically placed throughout the room. Mr. Hernández had not missed a detail!

The head table was situated so that the guests of honor could enjoy the view of the ocean through the glass panes directly in front of them. Three of the walls in the dining room were of glass, from floor to ceiling. The fourth wall connected the crystal room to the remainder of the hotel by means of two narrow doors from which waiters and waitresses entered and exited unobtrusively.

On one side of the room was a long series of rectangular tables where the food was being served. In the center of the table was a beautiful ice carving of a horse in flight with extended wings. Victoria had asked the artist why he did not stick to his original design of a runner with wings. "Too boring," he had responded. An artist's integrity was not to be questioned!

On the rectangular tables were silver containers and crystal bowls full of all types of cold and hot pasta dishes, vegetables, and salads. At one end there was a waiter carving ham, turkey, and roast beef. Another waiter served a light sole mernière surrounded by truffles and bathed in a white wine sauce.

It was a gorgeous evening. The sky was clear and full of stars. Dan Cole was hypnotized by the view from where he sat near the front. The wind must be blowing outside, he thought, observing the palm trees on the beach swaying gently from side to side. Everyone was dressed for the occasion.

As she entered the room, eyes turned to stare. Victoria stood motionless for a moment unaware that it was she who had silenced the crowd with her presence. She wore a satin green emerald dress that matched the embers of her green eyes. Her long brown hair cascaded down her bare shoulders and covered her back. Her jewelry was unpretentious. She wore a simple gold chain and diamond studs in her ears. Her face was clean and tanned with just a hint of mascara and blush. She wore a dark shade of lipstick for contrast.

"*Señora*, Mr. Bryan is waiting for you and has asked me to escort you to your table when you are ready," said Mr. Hernández.

"Thank you," she said in a low voice.

Dan couldn't take his eyes off of Victoria as she walked past him towards her table to greet the guests waiting for her.

*Had she seen him, he wondered? Had she known he would be there? How could he get her attention?*

"Victoria," Bryan whispered bending down to kiss her on the

head, "you look stunning tonight."

"You think so?" she smiled and thought about how she couldn't get her dress and shoes and hair to all cooperate until the very last minute.

"Yes! Every time I am away from you for a few hours, when I see you again, I am reminded of how truly beautiful you are!"

As the minutes became hours, and the hours seemed like years, Dan anxiously waited for an opportunity to speak to Victoria. There was so much he had wanted to say. People had surrounded her all evening. She had not been able to move from the main table since she had entered the room several hours ago. Finally she was alone at her table.

"Hello, Victoria?" he heard himself saying at last as he stood by her table.

She turned slowly and shook his outstretched hand. They paused awkwardly.

"Hello, Dan."

"May I have this dance?" he asked as people were beginning to swirl around the dance floor. Others had gone next door to the ballroom to watch the *Ballet Folklórico*.

Victoria was speechless. It had been so long. She felt like she had resolved all her past issues and insecurities in her mind, but now she only felt confusion as she stood facing him.

Dan led her to the dance floor and pulled her into his arms. She had a naturally clean smell and wore no perfume, just as he had remembered. He rested against her hair and held her tightly against his chest.

"Dan," she started.

"Shh. Please just dance with me."

The dance was over.

"Vicky, I need to talk to you alone. Can we walk along the

beach for a bit?" There was no harm in asking, but he feared the response.

"Sure," she had answered.

Victoria knew that they had to eventually talk for both their sakes. There were so many unanswered questions. She had rehearsed her questions over and over in case there had ever been an opportunity such as this. And yet, did the answers really matter anymore? Hadn't she continued on with her life and fallen in love with a man who returned her love without question? Wasn't Bryan everything she could have possibly wanted and needed? Then why would Dan's answers even matter?

"Have you ever been on a Cesna?" Dan asked her as they walked along the beach away from the hotel.

"A what?"

"A Cesna. It's a small plane. I went back and renewed my pilot's license."

"No, I haven't been on one," Victoria answered.

"You will be," he said.

"Dan, I haven't seen you in years, and you want me to *fly* somewhere in your *plane*?" she responded insolently. She hiked up her dress and started walking quickly back to the hotel. Dan burst after her and grabbed her arm causing her shoes to fall out of her hand and onto the sand.

"Victoria," he implored as she stopped to pick up her shoes. "*Marry me.*"

"*What?*"

"Please. Marry me."

"Dan, I thought you were engaged!"

"I was."

"I don't understand," she said.

"When I was boarding the plane in Arizona, I knew that I

wasn't coming here to represent my company and make a donation. I was coming here to get *you*."

"You broke up with your fiancée when you boarded the plane?!" she asked incredulously.

"I'm not proud of it. I hate hurting people. But yes, I broke up with her."

"Well you took an awfully big gamble thinking that I would just drop everything and run into your arms!" she retorted.

"Vicky, I don't *want* anyone else. If I can't have you, then I want no one."

"Please don't do this to me, Dan. I can't ..."

"If you say no, I won't ask you to marry me again. I will disappear from your life. All I ask is that you think about this, so please don't give me an answer right now."

"Dan we're just so different ..."

"That's it? You're worried because we're just different?" he asked with a little more hope now.

"I'm not the same person I was two years ago, Dan."

"Listen, have you ever been to the top of the Washington Monument?"

"Dan, this is silly."

"Really. Have you?"

"Okay," she said, "yes."

"What did you see when you looked down?"

"I saw people." She was getting annoyed.

"What else? Please, Victoria. You'll understand in a moment."

"I saw flags surrounding the monument." She closed her eyes to envision the scene that lay below. "I saw trees; some baby strollers. Maybe someone in a wheelchair." She slowly opened her eyes.

It was his turn. "I saw cars. Lots of them. And a police officer on a horse. An ambulance. And in the distance I saw the Duck."

"A duck?"

"No, *the* Duck. You know, it's that amphibian vehicle, sort of like a car-boat. Like at Normandy. It tours the streets of Washington and then drives right into the waters of the Potomac to get to the other side." The conversation seemed lighter now. He felt like he was getting somewhere.

"Dan, I have to get back..." she began saying.

"Wait. Let me explain. We have both been to the Monument; both looking down on the capital. But you saw things I didn't see. And I focused on things you didn't see. Our observations of our surroundings are different because *we* are different, not because the other variables don't exist! And yet, we both enjoyed the view, right?"

Victoria just looked at him. She was trying to understand.

"Your differences intrigue me and excite me, Victoria. They don't intimidate me. I don't feel repressed or rejected by them. I am drawn to you. It excites me to think about unraveling all the complicities that comprise Victoria; her memories, her dreams, her fears, and her expectations.

"Then why did you used to fight with me about those differ-ences so much, Dan?"

"I don't know," he answered honestly.

"Sometimes I felt as if we had been sculpting this big beauti-ful statue," she motioned with her hands. "And then every time we would fight, we would just knock the statue down piece by piece. Almost as if we were sabotaging its completion. It was exhausting, Dan!"

"I know. I know..."

"Why did you leave me, Dan?" she heard herself ask at last. She had been waiting for this response for two years.

"I didn't leave you. I made a mistake, and you left me. I let you go."

"You *let me go*? *YOU LET ME GO*?!!!" She was furious. "I *loved* you, Dan. You didn't need to *let me go*! You didn't even have the decency to call me and apologize, or at least explain what that lady was doing in your arms!"

"I did! And even if I had been able to reach you, would you have forgiven me, Victoria?"

"I don't know…" she said with tears in her eyes.

"You left the bracelet on the bridge. I thought that meant that you never wanted to see me again. But I did try to call, for what it's worth."

"It was probably just meant to be," she said recalling what Bryan had once said to console her about the end of her relationship with Dan.

"No, Victoria. I can't accept that. I love you."

"Who was the lady in your office?" Another unanswered question that Victoria had been keeping suppressed for two years.

"No one. She meant nothing to me. Can you please believe that?"

"Then why was she in your arms, Dan? I guess it was ironic that you were having an affair when you were having an affair!"

"I didn't sleep with her, Victoria. And I wasn't having an affair with you or her. You and I were separated from our spouses. Actually, my divorce had already gone through. Vicky," he repeated, "I didn't sleep with her."

"Dan, you *kissed* her. I mean, where do you draw the line? It's okay to kiss someone as long as you don't sleep with her? *We were in love!* We were committed. You told me that you had never kissed anyone the way you kissed *me*; that you had never made love to anyone the way we did. So what were you looking for that we didn't have?" Another unanswered question.

"I don't know…" he answered truthfully.

"*You don't know.* I was devastated, Dan. I thought of all kinds of reasons for what happened, and yet, *you don't know*. I thought I was undesirable, too fat, too short, too demanding of your time and affection. I analyzed every detail of every conversation I could remember with you just looking for clues. God, I didn't even know the name of my competitor," she threw her arms up into the air.

"Sandra," he said with his eyes cast to the sand.

"Sandra. How nice. But do you remember what you said to me that very morning when I woke up next to you in your bed? You asked me if I had taken an ugly pill with my vitamins. Do you remember?! Was I *that* ugly, Dan?"

"Victoria, I was teasing!" he implored. Dan knew deep down that he had said cruel things to her in the past. He didn't know why. Maybe he had been covering up for his own perceived deficiencies. Maybe he had been pushing her away for fear that he could never really have her. Or maybe he had just been trying to control her so that she would never leave him. It didn't make sense now. He wished he could take it all back now, all the awful hurtful things he had said to her over time.

"You said that I had ugly feet and that yours were perfect," she continued. "That I had wrinkles on my face and saggy breasts. You even made me go to a plastic surgeon to investigate making them smaller! You used to look at me in disgust in the car when the seatbelt pronounced my chest, so I would have to hold the belt with one hand to give the illusion that my chest was smaller."

"Victoria…"

"*I'm not finished*!" she screamed. "You wouldn't even let me wear turtlenecks, remember? No nude stockings, only white. No straight skirts, only pleated. And you would walk away from me in disgust if I wasn't wearing heels because you said I was too short for you. You said it made you look bad to stand next to such a short woman. *I'm not that short, Dan!* I'm five foot six for crying out loud! I flew home from that convention in San Francisco and ran through the gate to jump into your arms because I had missed you so much. And do you remember what happened? You got mad at me for wearing loafers instead of heels, and you told me I was insulting you!"

"Okay, okay! I know I said those things! But I don't think that way anymore, Victoria. You are a beautiful woman, just the way you are!"

"Dan, you hurt me with the things you said. They changed the way I think of myself. You destroyed my confidence. I have been working for a long time to get it back, and it hasn't been easy."

"I'm so sorry, Victoria."

"Sorry? Dan, I have just started to feel comfortable eating a meal in front of my boyfriend. I still have hang-ups about getting dressed in front of him. Do you know why? Remember how I used to go to your apartment sometimes after work, but we never had dinner together? It's because you couldn't watch me eat. You thought that I'd destroy my figure and the image you had of us together as the perfect couple. On the rare occasion that we went to a restaurant, I would have to order the light fare, and then stop eating as soon as you were done. I never had dessert. I never put a piece of candy in my mouth without disparaging looks from you. Do you understand what that has done to me? I wasn't even allowed to have a glass of wine, because it would make me an alcoholic. But you drank your glass of wine and said it was good for your circulation."

"Vicky," he said crying.

She was crying herself. The words were spilling out at such a rapid rate now, making up for all the years of repressed thought.

"*You made me feel ugly*, Dan. I couldn't even look in the mirror to put in my contact lenses because all I could see was ugly. But I *wasn't* ugly, Dan. Every time you would say something nice to me, you would take it away in the next breath by saying some-thing degrading. Why did you do that to me, Dan?" Her lips were trembling.

"I'm so sorry!" he continued crying.

"So am I, Dan. So am I. Because I did love you. But you threw my love away."

"No, Vicky. I didn't. I loved you too."

"You had a funny way of showing it. I thought we started off with such passion and understanding that first year. You admired me and my running, and you used to compliment me and you were proud of me. But somewhere along the line you started sending all these mixed messages. One time you even said that maybe we should be just friends. I was so naïve. So I decided to do just what you said, be friends, and give the relationship some breathing space. I started to look for the old me and who I was before I had met you. But I didn't even know who that old self was anymore! But I tried. I started focusing on friends and on advancing my career. That got your attention! It was as if you feared losing control of the ship if I ventured too close to the helm. You just couldn't let anyone else have my attention. You accused *me* of wanting someone else after it was *you* who pushed me away! You started telling me which friends I could associate with, and which of my friends you didn't want me talking to. I listened to you. What a mess I was!"

Dan looked at her incredulously. *Was all of this true? Had he done all of this to her without realizing it?*

"Bryan tells me that I am pretty. It doesn't matter what I look like on any given day; he tells me that I am beautiful. It has taken me all this time to understand that he is being sincere. Beauty is not about looks, Dan."

"Vicky, you *are* beautiful. You are the most beautiful woman I have ever known!"

"I'm not looking for a compliment, Dan! Don't you get it? I'm trying to tell you that love sees goodness and beauty in all the small things we do and say. I could be the ugliest person on this earth, and Bryan would tell me that I take his breath away!"

"Why didn't you tell me I had been doing all of this to you?"

"Was that my fault too? That I should have told you what you were doing?"

"No, no, Vicky. I didn't mean it that way."

"It wouldn't have mattered, Dan."

She turned and walked along the beach headed back to the hotel. He followed beside her.

"I have to get back now, Dan. I have a big race tomorrow."

She wished she could end on some positive note, because she knew that she had just ripped this man to shreds. No one deserves to be told all she had said to him and then receive no positive feedback at all for any of the good times they had shared. After all, it had really been her fault too for staying in a relationship for two years when she knew that it was not healthy for either one of them. She should have left long before she did. In any case, she just couldn't think of anything positive to say at that point. They continued to walk in silence.

"Was it that bad, Victoria?" he finally asked.

"It was confusing, Dan."

"Is there nothing left, then?"

"What do you mean?" she asked.

"Could you ever love me again?" he turned toward her and imploringly.

"Dan…"

"Please, Vicky. Don't answer tonight. I came here to ask you if you would marry me. I was going to ask you during the race."

"During the *race*?!" she laughed with more sincerity than sarcasm. "So you were really going to get down on your knees after running twenty-six miles and propose?"

"Well, more like *fall* on my knees, if I survive!"

They arrived at the hotel. Both stopped and looked at each other for a moment.

"I'm sorry about the lashing, Dan. I don't know where that all came from, but I guess it was just pent up for so long."

"I deserved it. Vicky, I really am a different person. Two years gives you a new perspective on life." He bent forward as if to kiss her, but she pulled away.

"Don't." Victoria knew that even an innocent kiss would be wrong. They were both too vulnerable. It had been a long day, and an even longer evening.

"Please think about my question," he said.

He took one of her hands in his and kissed it before walking away.

Victoria walked back to her hotel room feeling exhausted. She had no idea what time it was.

"It's eleven o'clock, Victoria. I was worried," said Bryan as he pulled her into his arms and searched for answers in her eyes. "You have a big race tomorrow morning."

She hadn't known that Bryan had been pacing for the past hour and calling her on the cell phone. But she had turned off her cell phone and had left it in her purse. Several people had told him that they had seen her walk towards the beach with one of the runners. Bryan knew in his heart which runner that would be. But he did not question Victoria's motives. He knew that she would have to eventually talk to this Dan fellow and set things straight in her mind. He loved her and trusted her implicitly. He just wished that he could help her, and he wondered if she was hurting.

"Let's go to bed, sweetie," he said to her. "Tomorrow is a big day for you."

He helped her take off her damp green dress speckled with sand and sat beside her on the other side of the bed.

"Goodnight, darling," he said kissing her on the forehead and pulling the covers up to her chin.

Victoria had still not said one word. Bryan walked into the living room, set the alarm clock, and tried to fall asleep on the couch. Victoria needed her time to think. She needed her sleep.

# CHAPTER THIRTY-NINE

Eight-thirty sharp, and all of the runners were on the line awaiting the command to begin the race. It was a beautiful day, just as had been predicted. There was a slight chill in the air, but the runners wouldn't feel that for long. The streets were lined with people cheering. The uplifting music that had been playing from large amplifiers had stopped. The Mayor was introduced, he said a few words, and then they were ready to begin the race.

"Two-word command," they heard the official announce. "Runners ready?"

Victoria was out in the front with about twenty seeded runners.

"MARK, GO!" The gun exploded into the air to mark the beginning of the race.

Bryan watched proudly as Victoria took off with the front of the pack. He had not slept much because he had been so worried about Victoria. He had finally just gotten up at five o'clock that morning and had gone downstairs to see if there were any details he had forgotten about for the event. Convinced that everything had been delegated and taken care of, he had gone in to wake up Victoria at seven o'clock.

Victoria had been upset about waking up at seven because she felt that it was so late. But Bryan knew that she had needed the sleep. He doubted that she had just fallen asleep right away after the events of the previous night. He still worried about her running this race, but he knew there was no sense trying to convince her otherwise. Bryan also knew that she would run the full twenty-six miles. She hadn't told anyone, but he had seen her registration card, and she had signed up for the full marathon. He was worried, but he was proud of her. He knew that this was something she had to do for herself. He just wished she could have felt enough trust to tell him. He never would have stopped her from running.

Victoria had gone out too fast for the first seven miles, and now she was trying to find her pace. Most of the seeded runners were trying to do the same. The *rabbits*, or pacers, had taken them out too fast. No one was very familiar with the territory since this was the first time a marathon had been run in the northern part of the island. There were hills and turns that had not received enough attention on the maps that the runners had studied.

The frontrunners did not know each other. They tried to figure out what the strategy would be for the front of the race. Was this one going to be a shoulder-runner and then pass on a curve? Should a runner drop back a bit and then surge on a hill? Who should have the advantage of the pace? Should a runner widen the gap in hopes that no one would challenge him until the end when they were all spent? When should the runner make a move?

By the tenth mile, Victoria had her pace. It was consistent, but not too predictable for others. They crossed a micro-chip mat. Several runners in the middle of the crowd had been running on the sidewalks and missed the mats. When they heard all the cricket-type chirps from the microchips attached to their shoelaces, the ones on the sidewalks ran back and crossed the electronic mats so that their times would be registered. If you missed a mat during the race, you were automatically disqualified. It would be assumed that you had not run the designated course and had cheated by taking a shortcut. No one had known where the mats were placed until that morning of the race.

As they approached the twelfth mile, Victoria started to get nervous. The course had made a loop to ensure that the half-marathon runners could veer off to the left and finish their race at 13.1 miles. The others running the full 26.2 miles would veer off to the right and begin another loop that would take them out further. Victoria was positive that she could stay strong for the full marathon. But she had told her family that she would only run thirteen. Victoria didn't know how her family would react when they saw her take the right turn to continue the race.

Christopher, Mayia, and Jennifer stood on the left side of the road slightly before the twelfth mile. They had all made posters to hold up as Victoria ran by. They had managed to get to the sixth mile marker, but they had missed her there. But they did make it to the twelfth mile marker without too much of a problem since it had looped around. There were four observation points set up so that spectators could cheer on their runners. Spectators probably couldn't get to all fours points and back to the finish line in time, but at least there were some options of places to go so that they could make it to a couple of the locations.

Victoria ran past her family and would have missed them again if it had not been for Gabrielle yelling out in her unmistakable French accent *"Vite! Vite! A la victoire, ma petite!"* Gabrielle had joined the kids just moments before Victoria ran by. Victoria managed a little smile and then continued her concentration so as not to break pace.

There was the fork. Left or right? *God, do I go left or right?* She continued right. She heard Jennifer scream "Go for it, mom!" She turned her head to the side to acknowledge her daughter's support and just wanted to cry.

They were at mile eighteen when Victoria heard Dan's voice behind her. "You're looking good!" he said as he pulled up beside her. Neither spoke. Victoria was in deep concentration, and she pushed all thoughts of Dan out of her mind immediately. He was just another runner. Dan was struggling to keep up.

A water station was approaching. Victoria veered off slightly to the right side of the street and passed the first two tables going straight for the third. She grabbed two glasses of the power drink and sloshed through the paper cups that already littered the street.

She gulped the drink down without stopping. No stopping; that was her rule. Too painful to get back into pace. Suddenly it seemed like there were people all around her and she couldn't find a break to get out of the crowd. *Shit, she should have never gotten close to the water tables!* She started to feel disoriented. A hand from the crowd pulled her out and back onto the road; it was Dan. She was back on the road and started running faster so as to make up the precious seconds she had lost back in the crowd. She found her running pack and returned to her pace with the female seeded runners. She knew she wouldn't be able to finish with them, but she'd try to keep up for as long as she could. Dan dropped back considerably and could not keep pace with her pack. That had been his spurt, and he had known it, but at least he had been able to see Victoria and help her out of the confusion at the water table.

At the nineteenth mile the pack passed a female runner kneeling at the side of the road rocking back and forth and crying. She had hit the wall. Not literally, of course. But the runner had not paced herself well. Victoria knew what that was like. It was more painful not finishing the race than the physical pain itself. You recover from physical pain, but you do not recover from quitting. She crossed another electronic chip mat.

Mile twenty. The medic's tent was up ahead and the sign said 'Dead runners over here.' Not funny. She'd have to find out whose idea that was from the committee. Her hip started to hurt. The pain went down her leg all the way to her toes. *Concentrate*, she told herself.

Approaching mile twenty-two, Victoria felt a wave of nausea come over her. Not enough water, she thought. Her breathing became erratic. Suddenly she started throwing up. Victoria ran over to the side of the road, turning her head as she vomited, but never stopping. Once you stop, you feel like you have hit a concrete wall. Victoria kept pushing to the next water table. She took two glasses. She drank the first one and threw up again. After a few seconds she drank the second one. It stayed down this time.

She felt a little better. Moments later she saw an extended arm from the crowd of spectators on the side; someone who was offering another glass of water. It was Christopher! She grabbed the glass, smiled at her son, and drank. Better. Much, much better. She stopped slapping her feet on the ground and regained her composure. *Butt forward, hips tall,* she could hear coach Carl saying back when she was training for the Olympics.

"Twenty-three" she heard the race marshal shout. A man next to her suddenly grabbed his hamstring and let out a dull moan. He dropped out of the pack and went to the side. *Focus,* she told herself looking straight ahead with an expressionless face.

"Twenty-five," she soon heard. Victoria quickened her pace. There were several female runners packed together, and they all knew that this was where the race would *really* begin. One point two miles, and they would know if they were in the top ten. The first five women were already way ahead of them, and they could still see the sixth and seventh place female runners about forty or fifty meters in front. Then Victoria and four other women were running shoulder-to-shoulder.

"*Corre, Victoria!*" she heard a spectator yell. Less than a mile now. Hundreds of people lined the sides of the road. The runners weren't being nice anymore. They wore stone cold faces. This is the competition. You could hear their breathing in front, beside, and behind you. You could even hear them get up on their toes for the final kick. Victoria was in pain. Every bone, every muscle, even her hair hurt!

Victoria blocked out everything around her and envisioned the finish. She focused straight ahead. Now there was no feeling, no emotion, and no pain. Just pure determination. She straightened her hips, pulled with her arms, and flew on her toes.

The crowds were getting louder, but Victoria could only hear what was in her head. Almost there. Half a mile. She sped up. The two women behind her also sped up. Eyes fixed, she was breathing hard. People were yelling from the sidelines. Victoria's one leg felt

CHERYL HOLDEFER

numb, but she opened her stride and pulled harder with her arms. One woman couldn't keep up and she backed off, but the other one managed to pull up beside her.

There's the curve at the end. *Get to the inside*, she told herself. One hundred meters now. She secured the inside of the curve to get the edge she needed. The woman directly behind her had had the same idea. So did another male runner. Before she knew what was happening, the three runners collided and fell to the ground. The man quickly rolled over to the side of the road at the curve to let the other runners pass, and then he got right back on his feet. Victoria and the other woman were still down.

Victoria opened her eyes but was disoriented. *"GET UP, MOM!"* she heard Jennifer scream in the distance. No one could interfere. That was the rule. No one could physically help the top ten runners.

The other woman was almost up. Victoria rolled over and onto her knees. One leg up. She pushed off the ground with her hands and was back on both feet. She could see the finish line, and she could see the other woman slightly ahead of her. There was gravel stuck in her knees as they bled, and her arms were scraped badly. Blood was running down from her forehead into her eyes. She was having a hard time focusing. She felt faint.

Twenty-five meters. Victoria was right beside the other woman now. They were both in pain, both pushing with every ounce of determination. Victoria pulled ahead of the other woman. Twenty meters. Fifteen. Suddenly Victoria faltered and dropped to one knee.

Bryan watched from the tower at the finish line. He was helpless. There was nothing he could do, nothing he could say. He couldn't show preference by encouraging her on the loud speaker either. He pushed the microphone into the hands of a colleague and jumped down the steps of the metal tower. *Please, God*, he said over and over again. *Please let her be okay!*

"Get up!" her friend Gabrielle yelled as loud as she could

198

from the side of the road. "GET UP, VICTORIA!"

The other woman had just passed her, but when she heard Gabrielle yell Victoria's name, the other runner turned suddenly.

"I didn't know it was you!" she said to Victoria who was trying to stand on two feet. "Get up! I know you can do this!"

"Go finish!" Victoria responded to the runner. "Go!"

"You have to do this for all of us!" the woman responded.

And Victoria did. They barely made it to the finish line before the next female runner closed in on them.

Victoria and the woman she had just spoken to were side-by-side. They were reaching the chute at the end. Victoria suddenly stepped behind her adversary forcing the other woman into the chute before her to win tenth place overall for women finishers.

The two women turned to each other in the chute and embraced. They saw the man who they had tangled with in front of them in the other chute and they leaned over the ropes to shake hands. All three of them were a mess, but they were laughing all the same! The medics were waiting for them at the end of the ropes.

"*Gracias*, Victoria," the other woman said as they reached the end of the chute.

"Wait! Tell me your name!" Victoria said to the woman with whom she had competed to the last second.

"Esperanza," the woman responded with a smile.

# CHAPTER FORTY

Victoria was greeted at the end of the chute by her family and friends who kissed her and hugged her and laughed and cried. Bryan lifted her up into his arms and carried her to the medical tent.

"Eleventh!" he exclaimed. "That's my girl!" he said looking down at her in his arms with his warm brown eyes. He couldn't have been more proud of her at that very moment. He would have been proud of her even if she had not finished, he thought. "You're the best, Victoria!"

Bryan loved her. He absolutely adored her. He knew early on when he met her that he had wanted to spend the rest of his life with her. But Bryan knew there was a possibility that he could not have her; that she belonged to someone else who had met her first four years before he had. As much as Victoria had returned his love and told him that she loved him, Bryan knew that it would not be complete until she had her closure with Dan. And that was what Bryan had been praying for this weekend, a miracle.

"Mom!" Jennifer ran into the tent with Christopher and Mayia close behind.

"Hi, sweetie!" Victoria's eyes filled with tears as she hugged her daughter and then her son and Mayia.

"Mom," exclaimed Jennifer, "three hours, five minutes, and twenty eight seconds!" Jennifer was jumping up and down as she said it.

"Ouch!" Victoria whined as the paramedic pulled gravel out of her bloodied knee with tweezers. She was laughing and wincing at the same time.

"Victoria Taylor?" asked another medic in the tent as he approached her.

"Yes?"

"Someone is asking to see you," said the volunteer paramedic. They were only allowing in family members so that the tent wouldn't get so crowded and they could attend to the patients.

"Must be reporters," Jennifer concluded. The small crowd moved away to the other side of the tent so that Victoria could have a few moments of privacy for her visitor. Bryan left the tent to find Gabrielle and to check on the race proceedings.

Several minutes later, Victoria saw him standing in front of her. It had not been a reporter. "Hi, Dan. How did you do in the race?" she asked.

"I did okay, but you did great today, Vicky; just great!" he answered.

"You think?" she beamed.

"Yes."

Victoria thought she saw a trace of a frown. "What is it, Dan? Are you okay?"

"I heard you gave up your place at the last second to another runner. You should have been tenth, Vicky. I don't want anyone thinking my wife is a quitter!"

# CHAPTER FORTY-ONE

Bryan had been entering the tent when he saw Dan lean down and hug Victoria. He saw the look of satisfaction on Dan's face as he looked up and saw Bryan. Victoria was turned away from him. *That was it*, Bryan thought. If she had chosen Dan, he would do his best to support her decision and would back out of the picture. He didn't want to make this difficult for her. He slowly backed up and walked towards the entrance of the tent to leave. He would go and finish his duties at the tower for the race, and then he'd pack up his bags and leave Puerto Rico as soon as he could. He wouldn't need to stay for the awards ceremony and the festivities after the race, because there were other people handling all of those responsibilities.

Christopher caught Bryan as he was leaving the tent. "Bryan, I don't think it's what it looks like," he said.

Bryan smiled at him and put his hand on Christopher's shoulder.

"I knew all along that the ending could be sad," Bryan paused, "but I guess I was just postponing reading the last chapter in hopes that someone had rewritten the words."

Bryan turned and looked at Victoria one last time over at the far side of the tent. She had never seen him.

"Take care of her, Chris. Your mother is one hell of a woman!" Tears came to his eyes. Christopher reached out and they hugged, and then Bryan left the tent for the last time.

Jennifer and Mayia had been watching the exchange from the side. They walked up to Christopher and each put an arm around his waist. All three of them watched in silence through the tent opening as Bryan disappeared into the crowd of runners and spectators.

At that moment they saw Gabrielle approaching the entrance of the tent holding out a bottle of champagne and some paper cups.

"Allow me," Christopher said to Gabrielle and took the bottle out of her hands. As he opened the bottle, the other three hugged and began exchanging stories of what they had seen from their vantage points on the race course.

Mayia indicated to Gabrielle that perhaps Victoria needed a few more moments alone with Dan in the corner where a medic continued to clean up her wounds. Then they would go and share some champagne with her and celebrate her victory. It had been just that: a victory, a dream come true, an exercise in confidence.

"Jennifer, why so sad?" asked Gabrielle as they stood there pouring the champagne to have a toast of their own before approaching Victoria and Dan.

"Just a lot of emotion around here today, you know?"

Jennifer was growing up so quickly, thought Gabrielle. "Listen, I have a plan that will cheer you up," she exclaimed.

"Aunt Gabi, I don't think I should dye my hair red," she said smiling at last.

"*Alors, non*! I have a *better* plan! But you know, a few reddish highlights would…"

"Aunt Gabrielle!" and now she was laughing.

"Okay, so you know what I am thinking?" Gabrielle ventured.

"I'm afraid to ask!"

"I am thinking that for Christmas in two weeks we should all go to Paris to celebrate!" her mom's friend said.

"Are you *kidding*?!"

"Why not? We can go to the shops at the Champs-Elysées and the Christmas markets near the Saint Sulpice Church. And then we can drive to the Arc de Triomphe at night where the streets are lined with beautiful illuminated trees. Oh, and we must not forget the Eiffel Tower! I will book us a river cruise and then we can eat lunch at the Tower! It is open until eleven o'clock at night, did you know?"

"That would be so exciting, Aunt Gabrielle! What do you think the chances are that mom would say yes?!"

"She looks very happy over there. Maybe she will say yes?"

Gabrielle thought that Victoria actually didn't look happy at all. She knew her friend. Something was going on, and she decided it was time her friend had a well-deserved vacation. Somewhere far away. So why not Paris?

The four continued to huddle in excitement, and Christopher made sure they all had a paper cup for the celebratory toast.

"To mom's victory today, and to Paris at Christmas!" They raised their glasses in agreement and sipped the champagne.

Jennifer turned around and headed to the medic's corner where her mom had been, but she wasn't there anymore.

"Have you seen my mom?" she asked the medic who had bandaged Victoria's knee and forehead.

"Yes. She said she was going out to watch the race. She left just one moment ago," he said pointing in the direction he had last seen Victoria.

Jennifer wondered how they had missed her because there was only one way to enter or exit the tent. They must have been celebrating too much without her!

Gabrielle was a step ahead of Jennifer and had seen Victoria leave the tent. She ran after her and caught up. After a few exchanged sentences and some laughter, Victoria took off again.

"Bryan!" Victoria yelled up at her assistant race director who was standing in the tower monitoring the last hour of the race.

Bryan looked down and hesitated. He wondered how he would get through the conversation they were about to have. But he had known that Victoria would want to talk; he just hadn't expected it to be at this moment. She would want closure with him, and he would give her time to get it. She was a decent person and would want to explain things to him.

He climbed down from the tower. Before he could even reach the bottom, he heard her yelling up at him.

*"Have you ever been to Paris in December?"*

"Excuse me?" he responded confused.

*"Paris.* I think you should come to Paris with me and my family for Christmas, because I'd like our first Christmas together to be one we will remember forever."

# CHAPTER FORTY-TWO

It was December 24$^{th}$, and Victoria's family was gathered around a large mahogany table at the home of her friends Gabrielle and Jean-Louis on the outskirts of Paris, France.

They had all just returned from the Cathedral of Notre Dame on the Ile de la Cité in the middle of the Seine River. They were getting ready for the *Réveillon*, or the traditional meal one eats after the Midnight Mass. There were toasts being made with champagne and *vin chaud,* as Gabrielle and her husband brought in the *foie gras* and the oysters with sausages.

After a meal of capon with chestnut stuffing, Victoria and Bryan stepped out onto the balcony for a few minutes while the others got ready for the dessert, *Buche de Noël.*

They could see shimmering lights from the city in the distance as the black night enveloped them in the cold winter air. Bryan put his arms around Victoria.

"So does this family of yours have a tradition of opening at least one present on the 24$^{th}$, or do you wait until the morning of Christmas?" he asked.

"We try to wait until the next morning, but sometimes we cheat!" she said.

"Either way, it is past midnight, so I'd like to give you your gift now."

Bryan pulled out of his pocket a small blue velvet box and put it in her hands.

Victoria stared at the box in her hands and finally looked up at Bryan's face.

"Go ahead and open it," he whispered.

She opened the box and found inside a white gold halo pave diamond ring with tiny diamonds surrounding the center.

"Will you marry me, Victoria?"
"Yes!" she said, with all her heart.

CHERYL HOLDEFER

# ACKNOWLEDGMENTS

I would like to thank my husband, Dave, for his infinite patience, for his help with putting this novel to print, and for providing such a fun and exciting life of adventures! I never know what is around the corner...

I would also like to thank Laura Fary and Bettan Sandström who were the first to read this novel and who encouraged me to publish it.

To my brother and sisters, I love you all. Some of you will recognize your characters in the book. Hope you like them!

Megan Tomás, thank you for the honor of being Godmother to your adorable daughter Emily. I hope I can be a "Rina" or "Gabrielle" to her when she is a teenager, and I promise not to let her dye her hair green for the prom! Love you both!

# ABOUT THE AUTHOR

Cheryl Holdefer resides in Columbia, Maryland, with her husband Dave and their four children. She is a former Spanish and French teacher, an associate professor, and is currently an assistant principal at a local high school in Maryland. She grew up in Puerto Rico and Denmark prior to attending college on the mainland. Cheryl's experiences as a former marathon runner, coach, and race director add to the credibility of Victoria's journey in her novel.

www.ingramcontent.com/pod-product-compliance
Lightning Source LLC
Chambersburg PA
CBHW060144130626
46556CB00006B/2489